The Second Life of Monsieur the Devil

The Second Life of Monsieur the Devil

H. Bedford-Jones

WILDSIDE PRESS

Published by
Wildside Press
www.wildsidepress.com

CHAPTER I

The Hidden Eye

THE pool of sweet water glowed like a round bit of the sky, a round mirror that reflected the clear cerulean blue which the Ch'ien-lung artists hit exactly, and which the K'ang-hsi artists missed with their greenish tinge.

Fifty feet was the diameter of that circle. About it, on all sides save one, ran a thirty-foot strip of white sand, unstained and beautiful as snow. On the one side was stretched an awning of coral-striped canvas, warding the tropical sear of the burning sunlight. Behind this canvas, leading down to it, was an avenue of trees; a thick, green, shady avenue, carpeted with the same white sand, walled by the pineapple-like trunks and the interlaced pinnate fronds of the palms. Under this hot sun *Phoenix canarensis* throve mightily, and the avenue formed a corridor walled and roofed in green, through which the sun-rays pierced in a tiny lace-work of golden meshes, but robbed of all their strength and heat.

Round about this white sand circle rose a twenty-foot wall of weathered pink stucco. This circular wall was broken by many odd projections and ledges, over which had been trained climbing roses. Just now, the wall was a mass of rich pink foliage that shut out all the world — or seemed to. The only break in this wall was where the avenue of palms lay like a streak of greenish-black shadows pointing away from the pool. On the side opposite this break, was a gate in the wall, a gate as solid as the wall itself. Thus, within this wall was a little world, and the wall shut out all the horizon, and the sea, and those who might intrude upon the little world within.

Yet, in the back of Sigurd was a tiny space the size of a leaf where the magic blood of Fafnir had not touched; and by this tiny space came the hero to his death. Likewise in this wall was a gate, and in this gate, which was seldom opened, was a tiny keyhole.

A single swimmer was disporting herself in the pool, making evident its depth by her long dives. She was no marvelous swimmer; still, she enjoyed this pool with the whole-hearted abandon of one who relaxes absolutely to the pleasure of the moment.

Against the rippling blue of the water, her body glowed golden. A cap of yellow rubber bound her hair. Tired of swimming, she turned upon her back and floated idly, her figure half revealed, half hidden by the lapping wavelets, her eyes rapt upon the blue sky above. Staring thus into the depths of the sky-bowl, she lay motionless, and presently lost her poise in the water, as one will. Quietly her staring eyes went down under the fluid.

A splutter and cough, and her body flashed. She laughed at her own mischance, and struck out for the shore and the canvas awning. Behind the keyhole, in the gate, came a slight and insignificant flash; as it were, the flash of the sun upon a black and glittering eye which moved to follow her.

THE girl came to the shore, and stood up. For a moment the sunlight bathed her figure, painting it a pure golden hue, vibrant and delicate of outline. Then one saw that she was clad in a skin-tight vesture of golden wool — a suit that clothed her slender shape like a glove, revealing every swelling outline, every exquisite curve and shape. Her bare feet splashed in the shallows, and she flung herself forward into the shade of the awning, gathering the warm white sand in about her hips.

For a space she sat there motionless, hands clasped about her knees, gazing at the sky and the pink wall and the blue pool. Suddenly she glanced at the empty avenue of shade, as though moved by some inward impulse. Her hand crept to the shoulder-strap that bound her vesture, and she unbuttoned it. One could easily comprehend the impulse, in this spot so shut away from all the world, to be free of all clinging garments and to plunge gloriously into that blue pool of the sky!

Her one shoulder bared, the girl suddenly paused. There had been no faintest sound, no stir of the warm and listless sunlight; yet she paused, her eyes roving about. One would have declared that she was startled by no physical thing, but by some spiritual intuition. Her gaze dwelt for an instant upon the gate opposite her. It was impossible that she should detect the minute glitter at the keyhole, yet slowly she buttoned the shoulder-strap again. A shrug of her shoulders and she stood up, plunged into the pool, and swam straight across it to the farther side. There she landed and walked up to the gate. She did not attempt to open this, but set her bare feet in the rough stucco and ascended the wall like a golden flame. Her head rose above the ornamented top of the wall; she clung there a moment, watching, a slight frown clouding her clear features.

No one was in sight.

Beyond the wall was ground, solidly sown with tight clusters of lipia-grass, like a greenish gray carpet. Here and there were set trees, in round places cleared of grass; mangoes, clad in massy pink blossom, their leaves like wine-hued ribbons; limes and oranges, scenting the air. A queer medley of trees, here! One or two flame-trees, blood-red in the sunlight, were mingled with the fat deep greenery of figs. And amid the mangoes was that tree with the most rare and wonderful of all tree perfumes, the Chinese magnolia, ivory petals ready to fall.

Around these trees one glimpsed a thick pomegranate hedge, while water ran in rivulets from some hidden source, following channels which seemed haphazard yet which were deeply grooved — the rains were long since over, and a little irrigation hurt nothing. A hundred feet distant, the land dropped sharply away in a thin, sword-like line, and beyond it appeared the sea-horizon. That drop was very abrupt and startling. There was no shore; nothing, in fact, but fifty feet of cliff, with the ocean at the bottom. A strange place, this, beneath the tropic sun!

The girl beheld no living thing in sight, although many men might have lain concealed there before her; and one, in fact, did so lie. She dropped back from the wall into the white sand, swam across the pool again, and came to land. Beneath the awning, she picked up a robe of gossamer silk, wrapped it about her shoulders, and walked up the shady avenue of palms. The frown had vanished from her face, and she sang light-heartedly as she walked.

IN THE garden orchard over which she had just gazed, the brown figure of a man arose from the thick hedge. This man had some excuse for hiding himself, since he was stark naked. The sun had burned him much. Over his head was a thatch of dark red hair, white with brine from the sea-water. His face was flat, broad, powerful without being refined; the black eyes glittering beneath dark reddish brows were alight with an incredible intelligence and energy. His body was bony from hunger and suffering, drawn by long immersion in water, yet very muscular.

This man crept to the gate in the wall and peered through the keyhole. He rose again, a grin upon his lips, and hastened to the nearest rivulet of water. He flung himself down and drank thirstily. Rising, he drew his hand over his lips and glanced at the sun.

"Nine o'clock!" he muttered. "All morning climbing that cliff!"

He cast a malevolent glance toward the cliff and the horizon. Something in his words, in his look, in his appearance, conveyed the idea that he had come out of the sea below and was now exulting over it in a fiercely triumphant hatred. Yet, to have come from the sea, he must have come from some other land — and there was no other land in sight.

When he turned about, one saw that over his naked back, like grids, ran the faint meshes of scars that could have come only from many whippings under the lash. When he walked, it was seen that to a very slight degree *"il claudiquait,"* as the French say — he showed that he had trailed ball and chain behind him.

On one side of him was that cliff. On two sides were pomegranate hedges, behind which appeared rank tropic shrubbery, with no semblance of order. The irrigating water was a constant seep from the swimming pool, which was therefore fed by underground springs.

On the fourth side was the wall, and to this the man turned. He tried to open the locked gate, but its massive strength resisted him. He tried to climb the wall, but fell back and lay in the sand, exhausted by the slight effort.

"Done up!" he muttered. Suddenly his eyes shone. "There must be a house, eh? Then there must be boats. Done up? Not yet!"

He came to his feet and laughed. That laugh was an effort of the will. He went to the wall, covered on the outside with roses, and searched among these vines. Presently an exclamation of satisfaction broke from him. He stood erect, holding a bit of wire which had been used to fasten the original vines in place.

With this wire he went again to the gate, and

stooped to the keyhole. In two minutes he touched the gate and it swung open.

He stepped through, closed the gate carefully, and flung himself toward the pool of fresh water, and the avenue of shading palms beyond.

MEANTIME, at the other end of this avenue of palms, was being enacted a quaint idyl in the frailty of human nature and one's affectionate regard for the muse of science. Who was this muse of ethnologic philosophy, by the way? I, for one, do not know. Yet it is high time that she were tracked down, discovered, named; in these latter days she has many devotees. It is to be doubted if she had any more faithful devotee, however, than Jean Marie Auguste des Gachons.

Once upon a time, and not so very long since, Des Gachons had been a high official in that great colonial realm of France which began with an expedition into Indo-China, reached out grasping fingers until Cambodia on the south and Tonkin on the north were enclosed, stretched forth a thumb into Siam and a little finger into Yunnan, and gripped at an empire.

A high official in this empire has many chances at wealth, and Des Gachons thoughtfully neglected none of them. He was a gentle soul, hating the army and colonial politics. When his wife died, and his brother was killed in Tonkin, Des Gachons took his pile and withdrew to devote his life to science and his daughter. And, one must admit, he had chosen a very pretty place for his devotions.

Here was an island, where he reigned as absolute

monarch and owner. Crowning this little island, he had built a great rambling house in French Colonial style, where he dwelt with his daughter and his two secretaries, his French gardener, his French chef and boatman, his native servants. Here he was a little emperor, and here he could grow fat and wise in perfect bliss.

Berangère, having dressed after her swim, sought this father of hers. She turned from the wide, shaded colonnade before the house, and passed into the sunken gardens. Here, now that the rains had subsided, Des Gachons had transferred his library and his atelier, into the open air.

The girl paused at sight of the scene which greeted her, a light smile touching her lips.

A small amphitheater had been planted with limes and Chinese magnolias. These trees had been trimmed very high, so that they formed a shady roof over the place — a roof from which was wafted the rarest of perfumes. Below were tables, typewriters, Singapore chairs, a huge round gong to summon servants.

Here sat Des Gachons. He was a great fat man, dreamy of eye, tender of heart, his beard trimmed into two long prongs. He was very vain of this beard, which, in conjunction with his elaborately curled mustaches, gave him the deceptive appearance of a very Porthos. The desk beside him was littered with papers and note-books. At a portable bookcase one young man was diligently searching for some item. Another young man was seated, taking in shorthand the stream of wisdom which flowed from the master's lips. These two secretaries, naturally, were desperately in love with Berangère, and might as well have been in love with the moon for all the good it did them.

At SIGHT of his daughter, Des Gachons struggled to his feet and bowed. He kissed her cheeks, and the two young men trembled. She dutifully kissed his cheeks, and the two secretaries turned pale. They bowed profoundly as she directed smiling greetings toward them.

"Mon père," she said, allowing Des Gachons to reseat himself and draw her upon his knee, "I must go to Saigon again, at once!"

The big man's brows uplifted in Gallic astonishment.

"So soon, Bergeronnette? So soon, when we have just returned to our charming home after spending the entire season of the rains in that little Paris —"

"Exactly," said the girl. "You see, all six of those frocks I had made, are absolutely impossible! I ordered the sleeves very short, to conform with the newest modes — after cabling to Paris in the matter, too! — and that assassin of a modiste has made them too long! So I must go and attend to it."

Des Gachons grimaced uncomfortably. "But, my tender little shepherd-girl," he said, lingering on the diminutive of her name, "but Bergeronnette, you perceive that I must finish this paper —"

Her shoulders lifted in a shrug. *"Tiens, donc!* I am

not going to interfere, *mon père.* I shall take old Paul, who keeps your fleet in order, and we may have the small cruiser, is it not? Three days, and we shall be in Saigon. A week there, and we return."

"Oh, if you insist! I shall have to go —"

"I refuse to permit it! Am I a child, then? Am I a silly little thing?"

"The good God knows you are not!" Des Gachons stifled a sigh. "But —"

"Never mind the rest." The girl stooped and planted a swift kiss upon his cheek. "Then we shall leave tonight —"

"If you will wait but two days," said Des Gachons, with the air of one who is resigned to the inevitable, "I shall have this paper completed, ready for you to mail from Saigon. It must reach the *Révue Archéologique* at the earliest date, for it completely refutes certain theories of the great Pelliot in the *Bulletin de —*"

"Very well," cut in the girl. "Very well. In three days, to give you an extra day of grace! Now I shall not interfere further with your work."

SHE withdrew. Des Gachons gazed after her with another of his heavy sighs. The two secretaries echoed the sigh.

"Should she go thus, unaccompanied?" ventured one of them, a mournful hope in his voice. Des Gachons darted a look at the speaker, then smiled dryly.

"*Mon brave,* when you can take care of yourself as well as this girl — *nom d'un nom!* I would like to see the man who can handle her! Heaven knows I cannot. Now, where did we leave off with those quotations —"

He resumed his work.

Berangère, meantime, followed a cement walk that led from the house amid its bowers of green; she descended this walk to its precipitous end. She came out upon a small terrace. Directly below her, at some thirty feet, was a small, perfectly enclosed harbor. At the edge of this harbor were boat houses. Anchored in the little port were a large motor cruiser, a smaller and faster model exactly like it, a schooner, tiny in size but perfect in detail. On the sand were a number of whale-boats.

The girl touched a lever at the edge of the cliff, and brought into view an escalier which was moved by an ingenious arrangement of counterbalanced weights. She stepped on to this and set it in motion. It deposited her upon the shore beneath, and from the boat houses appeared an old man wearing a Breton cap, who saluted her respectfully. Berangère danced up to him and kissed his brown cheek.

"In three days, Paul, we go to Saigon, you and I — with the little cruiser!"

"*Ciel!*" exclaimed the old seaman. "But —"

"*Pas un mot, Paul!*" exclaimed the girl. "Not a word! And listen: you know that papa was expecting a consignment of brandies from America? We shall bring them back, as a surprise!"

"Heaven knows," said Paul, with the grumbling air of one who is privileged, "there is a cellar full of liquor up above now! An army could not drink it all."

"Bah! If it pleases Papa, why not? He says that when all the world has gone dry, this island shall be an asylum for the next thousand years! In three days, remember!"

Paul nodded.

Neither the old Breton nor the girl perceived a slight movement upon the crest of the cliff above, nor the imperceptible glitter of a flashing eye.

Upon the following day, old Paul reported that one of the whaleboats had vanished from the lagoon. No one was missing from the island. The thing was inexplicable, unless the boat had been laid up too low on the shore, and had washed out with the tide. So, they concluded, it must have done.

CHAPTER II

Monsieur le Diable

SAIGON is a city consciously modeled, in general plan, buildings, streets and customs, upon Paris — that is to say, upon the Paris of a generation ago. One may find much in Saigon that is supposedly forgotten in Paris — even to very bad French.

For example, there is a certain Cabaret du Chat Gris, located in the lower part of the city, convenient to the wharfs and railroad and the Arroyo Chinois. Here, for a few cents, one may drink from divers fountains of evil. Here, for a few dollars, one may disappear forever. The cents largely predominate, naturally.

Five men were sitting about a table in the Gray Cat, fingering a greasy deck of cards and drinking execrable red wine. Le Brisetout was a huge uncouth monster of hair and flesh who worked in the nearby abattoir. L'Etoile, a fiery little devil of a man, wore a green patch over one eye; the other orb blazed like a star of green fire. Le Morpion was a human bulldog, bulging of brow and chin, a retired seaman whose hands were knotted and lumpy, and whose glittering little eyes were extremely dangerous.

The fourth man was different. He had come of a finer strain; even in his poverty and dirt he retained a certain grace, a certain debonnaire scoundrelism. His beard was somewhat trimmed, and one conjectured that he might have been a gentleman. His weary and dissipated features held a lingering suspicion of having once been handsome. He had the peculiar skin of one who eats opium, which was not intended by the Creator to be eaten by white men.

The fifth man was dissimilar to all these four. Like them, he was ragged, unkempt, prone to vicious words. His unshaven features were bony and rugged, his gray eyes were bloodshot. Unlike these others, he was neither French nor of mixed blood, but an American. He had drifted into Saigon, broke, and was working as a laborer at the Quai François Garnier.

Aside from these five at the table, two other persons were in the room. One was the proprietor, who was reading a newspaper across the bar. The other was a man with a dirty bandage about his jaw. He had entered, demanding wine and *"de quoi écrire,"* and sat at a table in a dark corner. Here, however, he wrote only briefly. He mainly watched the five gamesters and sucked at a long cheroot hungrily, as though drinking the nicotine into his very soul after long abstinence.

"Now, as for me," said L'Etoile in crisp argot, "I have been at honest work for six months — Laugh, fools, laugh! But it is true. When they took M. le Diable, and sent him to Noumea, I swore that I would turn to honest work until he escaped."

"Bah!" said Curel, he who might once have been a gentleman. "One does not escape from Noumea!"

"Exactly." Le Brisetout reached out hairy paws for the cards. "One does not! I know, for I have been there, me!"

There was a laugh. Smith, the American, looked up. "Who is this M. le Diable? I've heard you speak of him, but —"

"Yes!" Le Brisetout mouthed an oath. "Who is he, you? We know him not, in Saigon."

L'Etoile looked at Le Morpion. Between these two men passed a glance of singular meaning. It was Le Morpion who answered, as though in that glance he had read a command.

"Monsieur the Devil? Why, he is Monsieur the Devil — that is all! He is the king of all good rascals and honest thieves. They say that he was an artist, a man of talent, and that something happened to him. You know the crazy artists who lived on Tahiti for years? Something of the sort. At all events, one night in Shanghai — *croque!* And they had him. They brought him down here for trial and sent him to Noumea for life, the dogs! It was a betrayal."

"Yes," said L'Etoile with a certain mournful satisfaction, "it was a betrayal. But the man who betrayed us — I mean the man who betrayed him — confound this wine, it thickens the tongue! — Well, that man died very suddenly the next day."

"Good enough," put in Curel languidly. "I hope this M. le Diable escapes. I have heard of him. I would like to meet him. I think that he might break the monotony of life's facts."

LE BRISETOUT glared at the speaker in scorn.

"Escape? Bah!" he roared. "No one can escape from Noumea! All around in the hills are brown devils, armed with clubs shaped like — like — well, you know what, you! When one escapes, they beat him nearly to death, then drag him back. And, besides, one cannot swim a hundred miles."

"Ah! But M. le Diable can," said L'Etoile with conviction.

"Certainly he can," said the American. "I can myself. At least, if it were a question of escape from that hell, Noumea!"

The eyes of the bandaged man in the corner dwelt curiously on the face of Smith.

The cards were dealt. The five men fell to their game. Presently it was over, and Curel gathered in the pack. Le Brisetout stretched out one hairy, mammoth paw.

"A hundred miles!" he said, as though recollecting the former train of speech. "Ah! That is clearly impossible, M. Smith!"

Curel's voice cut in, a bit dreamily.

"I should like to meet this M. le Diable!" he reflected aloud. "Decidedly, the monotony of life is a fearful thing. The facts of life — you apprehend! One desires to get away from facts. How pleasant to be a Bolshevik and abolish all fact!"

L'Etoile, adjusting his green patch, laughed softly. That laugh was like the snicker of steel on steel.

"If you ever meet M. le Diable," he responded, "you will have no more monotony, my gentleman! As for your facts of life, I know nothing about them. You should have known our M. le Diable — a true artist! No gutter pickings for him. 'Cré nom!'"

"He was an Apache, perhaps?" queried Curel, dealing.

"Devil take me if I know," said L'Etoile frankly. "He spoke all tongues, had been all places. I have thought at times he might be American or English. One hardly asks him questions."

"I wish to hell he'd show up here, then," said Smith roughly. "If I could get away from this cursed town, I'd sell myself to the devil, man or fiend!"

Suddenly the voice of Le Brisetout boomed forth upon them.

"I say it is impossible!"

Smith looked at him. "What now, hairy ape?"

"To swim a hundred miles is impossible!" Rage flooded into the brutish features. "The man who says so lies, and is a —"

The epithet fell. Instantly Smith's arm flashed across the table and his fist struck Le Brisetout a blow which would have staggered any other human being. This human gorilla, however, only mouthed a curse and flung himself forward. His two immense, hairy paws gripped Smith by the throat. The table was hurled aside in the encounter.

Le Brisetout stood up, still gripping Smith by the throat, and shook him savagely. Then, with swift precision, the hands of the American crept upward. Each hand gripped a little finger of Le Brisetout. Smith gave a sudden heave of his shoulders and arms.

From the hairy giant burst a hoarse cry of agony. He flung his two hands about in the air, tried confusedly to wring them, cried out anew. Smith seized him by the shoulder and kicked him toward the door. Le Brisetout vanished in the street outside, whimpering and groaning. His two little fingers had been broken.

The proprietor turned his uninterested gaze to his newspaper again.

Smith rejoined his companions, laughing easily at their astonishment. Curel put forth a hand to him, with a gesture of pride. Caste, after all, does assert itself.

"Congratulations! It was well done, that; I am glad to be rid of the brute."

Smith nodded, then glanced at the other two. "You are not his friends?"

L'Etoile shrugged disdainfully, Le Morpion shook his bulging head.

"His friends? Hardly, my American! M. Curel was dealing, I believe?"

Smith bent to pick up the table. Suddenly L'Etoile, who was glancing at the bandaged man in the corner, turned pale as a ghost. This man had made an almost imperceptible gesture.

The bandaged man made another gesture, this time toward the proprietor — evidently asking if the latter were to be trusted. The jaw of L'Etoile fell. His pallor deepened, but he nodded assent.

From his seat in the corner rose the bandaged man, and stepped forward. He removed his wide hat, to uncover a shock of reddish hair. With a deft motion, he unwound the bandage from about his face. Le Morpion uttered one choking, inarticulate cry, and staggered back as from some awful apparition.

"M'soo — m'soo —"

"M. the Devil," said the stranger, bowing. "Messieurs, good evening!"

All four stood staring blankly at him. Smith glanced at the two rogues. In their stricken faces he read amazed recognition. It was impossible to doubt that the man before them was the same of whom they had been speaking.

THE proprietor quietly came from behind his bar, locked the door, and returned to his newspaper. He was, obviously, a discreet individual.

The silence continued. Smith was well aware of the audacity of this appearance, here in Saigon, the very hub and headquarters of French authority! This M. le Diable would be hunted like a wild beast the instant his escape became known, the instant his presence was suspected !

"When one swims a hundred miles," and M. le Diable smiled at Smith as though reading his thoughts, "one is naturally given up for dead! And I think," he added reflectively, "that it was something more than a hundred. Of course, I had assistance at first — a preserver lost from some ship. Providence must have sent it to me — or perhaps my namesake! Yes, decidedly, it must have been my namesake."

Curel bowed, a trifle mockingly, and spoke in cultured accents.

"Perhaps it is desired that I withdraw? One gathers that M. Smith and I may find ourselves *de trop* —"

"On the contrary," responded the other, in equally pure French, "I should be greatly pleased to cultivate your acquaintance, gentlemen."

Smith picked up the table and set it on its feet.

"The pleasure is mutual," he said. "Suppose we sit down."

Le Morpion and L'Etoile dropped into their chairs, still staring at this individual who had come from the dead — or worse, from Noumea!

M. le Diable seated himself. Under his thatch of reddish hair, glittered his black eyes. His broad, powerful features were filled with virile energy. He quite ignored his two former followers, and gave his attention to Curel and Smith. The bandage must have served him only as a disguise, for he was quite uninjured.

He spoke in English.

"I am glad we met. These two friends do not understand us, so speak freely," he said. His voice was level and poised, a voice of refinement and deadly reserve strength. "You first, M. Curel. From your recent conversation, I gather that you are wearied by the monotony of facts. And yet there must be some reason for that boredom, and for your presence here —"

Curel laughed. From his pocket he took a tiny box of opium pellets and laid it before him.

"The reason, M. le Diable? Behold it! In the days of my youth, I was given to liquor. I learned that one who took opium, entertained an aversion to liquor. Hence, to cure myself, I began to take opium in the form of pills. True, the liquor habit was cured; yet —"

M. le Diable threw back his head in a burst of hearty laughter.

"Come, this is rich!" he exclaimed, in tones which would have led Smith unhesitatingly to pronounce him an American. "Devil take me, but this is rich! One overcomes absinthe in order to become an opium fiend! Well, M. Curel, I believe you. This little incident of your career is one of those things which, although perfectly true, would appear incredible to most people.

"If I guarantee to relieve you from the monotony of facts, and place before you an adventure in which no sane man could believe, will you join me?"

"With all my heart," answered Curel.

"Agreed." Mr. Devil turned to the American. "Well, sir? How come you here?"

SMITH rolled a cigarette and surveyed his interlocutor whimsically.

"What is this, some Arabian Nights affair? If you want any facts from me, come across with some yourself, first."

"This is droll!" said the other, smiling. His smile betrayed vividly white teeth, queerly pointed, not unlike the teeth of those Africans who file their incisors to sharp points. His laugh was gay and infectious. "Droll! One man shrinks from facts; the other demands them!"

Suddenly he fell serious. "I might say that, before my somewhat enforced visit to Noumea, I instructed L'Etoile, who is a faithful soul, to await me at this place and to have with him two or three others. That you are here, is a recommendation, I assure you."

"Your assurance is a compliment," said Smith politely. "Who are you?"

Again the other smiled.

"What, still more insistence upon facts? My dear sir, you show little toleration of the modesty which M. Curel shows in the face of these naked facts! I presume you desire a name for me. Well, it would be convenient to have a name, I admit. Therefore I take the name of Lebrun, to be in harmony with the majority. A few moments ago you declared that you would sell yourself to the devil, my *Faustus* junior. Have a care! Such an invocation may well become an application!"

Curel interposed with a whimsical word.

"This goes well, M. le Diable, I assure you! We are certainly departing from all prosaic facts. I trust you do not claim to be the devil in person?"

"Some have thought so," responded Lebrun. His black eyes flashed with somber fire. "Have you any doubts in the matter, M. Curel?"

The other shrugged. "I? *Ma foi*, none! I am satisfied."

"Then, pray, do not interrupt." Lebrun turned to Smith. "Come! Yes or no?"

"To what?" drawled the American.

"To an alliance."

"Yes, if you like."

"Agreed. What brought you here?"

Smith puffed at his cigarette. "My feet in the first

instance," and he grinned. "In the second, lack of money. In the third, the interference of the police in my affairs."

"Ah!" Lebrun regarded him with satisfaction. "You are wanted?"

"Very badly wanted," said Smith.

"Shall you have a little money now —"

"I?" Smith shrugged his shoulders. "Oh, I have plenty!"

"The devil! But you just said the lack of money brought you here —"

Smith grinned at him. "Sure! The lack, you see, made me obtain some; the obtaining it, made me take to my heels; taking to my heels brought me here. Once here, I found it hard to get away. So I am working on the docks until my chance comes to slip aboard a ship."

"The police here are seeking you?"

"I don't know. In Tonkin, up north, they certainly are."

"Very well, gentlemen." M. le Diable assumed an air of business. "My usual custom is to take one-half the proceeds of our business, and to divide the other half among those who aid me. There will be you four, and a fifth, a lady. No more. Is this satisfactory?"

BOTH Smith and Curel indicated their assent. Lebrun turned to L'Etoile and Le Morpion, and changed his tongue to the argot they spoke.

"Do you remember, you, the name of the excellent

gentleman who sentenced me to spend the rest of my life in Noumea?"

L'Etoile, by far the more adroit of the two rascals, made prompt reply.

"It was Des Gachons — his approval of the papers was almost his last official act. We have often regretted that he left the country before we could interview him."

"It is just as well." Lebrun smiled grimly. "Do you know where he is?"

"No."

"But I do." He rose. "Come with me. You others follow, but not too closely."

All five of them politely bade the proprietor good night, and issued forth into the street. Smith and Curel were the last to leave. In obedience to the orders of Lebrun, they waited in order to give the other three a slight lead.

At this instant, the American felt his companion touch his arm significantly.

"Damnably clever!" said Curel in English.

"Eh?" Smith glanced at him. "What do you mean?"

"Nothing. Only that I happen to recognize you. I remember you now."

Smith laughed. "So? I'm afraid you are mistaken."

"As you like. Only, I am very sure that I saw you two months ago, in Hué City, under somewhat different circumstances than these."

Smith started. "The deuce you did! Then —"

"My dear Smith," and Curel laughed softly, "why

be alarmed? My interest in such a game as this gives me something to live for. Two hours ago, I strongly contemplated suicide. Now, I am eager, full of the *joie de vivre!*"

"I congratulate you," said Smith dryly. "None the less, I fear you are mistaken."

"As you prefer. But I bear by right a `de' before my name. My ancestor rode to Egypt with Joinville. I think you are no longer alarmed concerning what I know?"

"I never have been," said Smith cheerfully. "One may be surprised, but not alarmed. Only, if you hinted it to Lebrun —"

"It would make trouble?"

"For Lebrun, perhaps."

Curel laughed heartily. "You have an astonishing self-confidence! But I shall say nothing of it. I repeat, the game interests me. I have never delved deeply into crime, but now I am grateful for the opportunity. It will be absorbing! You have my promise."

"Your word's good with me. Come along — I don't want to lose the others!"

The two started after their companions.

CHAPTER III

The Engaging of Félice Bonnard

WHEN Berangère des Gachons arrived at Saigon, the government had departed for Hanoi for their six-months' residence in the north, and she had the southern capital pretty much to her own sweet self. She made the most of it.

No longer was the absence of "the court" regretted, no longer was the pleasant city dull and lifeless. The Rue Catinat picked up in business, and the Boulevard Norodom witnessed the amazing sight of government clerks hastening to work and hastening away. In effect, Berangère not only demoralized the *Palais*, but the city itself. Brought up in official life, she had no awe of the chiefs of *bureau*, and if she wanted a trifle of help in a customs affair or any such petty detail, she came straight to the Palais du Gouvernement and cut the red tape.

Berangère was apt to be impetuous, although it must be admitted that she had a way of converting over-hasty impulses into triumphs on the approach of disaster. It had occurred to her that if she provided another objective for the sheep's-eyes of the two secretaries at home, she might save herself a good deal of annoyance. Accordingly, on the second day of her visit, there appeared in *L'Opinion* an advertisement which stated that she desired a maid.

Many maids, Eurasian, French and native, sought admission to her rooms at the Continental, but none were chosen. At length appeared Félice Bonnard.

It was morning when this application came. Berangère had breakfasted in her room. She was arrayed in a *robe de chambre* of gorgeous deep yellow, with boudoir cap to match; she had a penchant for this hue, which well set off her own golden yellow hair, her deep blue eyes, her vivacity of color. When Félice entered, she perceived at once that she had found her maid.

This Félice was a woman of twenty-odd, very chic, a decided brunette. Her mournful dark eyes held a fund of experience. They were dangerous, those eyes. They marked their owner as one who knew much of the world from varied angles. Her dress betrayed remnants of taste — real worth fallen upon days of poverty. Berangère saw before her what would be termed in England a "gentlewoman in reduced circumstances."

"Ah!" she exclaimed, motioning to a chair. "You are not exactly the type one would expect to see, Mademoiselle."

"Madame," corrected Félice, smiling a little. Her smile was most attractive. "Madame Bonnard, Mademoiselle. My husband was an officer in the army, and was killed at Verdun. We had been married only three months. After that, I nursed. At length I heard of a fine opening here, and came. Now I am in trouble with the authorities, because they do not wish nurses and since I have no family they say I must go back to France. The opening did not develop. I have no money and no friends. If I could get a position of any sort —"

"Listen," said Berangère. "I wish a maid, you comprehend? You have pride —"

"When one has nursed the poilus, Mademoiselle, one has no pride; that is, no pride in the old sense. Only pride that one has been of service."

Well, that was a good answer. It captivated Berangère. She perceived that this woman would have the two secretaries fighting a duel within a fortnight.

"I live on an island," she said. "There is little companionship. You will be lonely. We spend the rainy season each year here in Saigon. For the remainder of the time, we live on the island by ourselves. We have few visitors, no social life. Consider!"

Félice smiled. "Mademoiselle, I have much to forget."

Berangère nodded and rose. "Come back this afternoon at three."

W HEN her visitor had departed, Berangère dressed and summoned a 'riksha. She was whirled out the Boulevard Norodom to the palace, and there impressed an eager and attentive clerk into service.

She started a train of inquiries that took them to the Commissariat Central, then down to the Customs and Revenue office on the quay, and finally ended at the government office in the Rue Lagrandière. Here a smiling official spread before the young lady a *dossier* which related to the Veuve Bonnard.

"But," said Berangère, "there is then nothing wrong with her?"

The official spread his hands. "Nothing. But we do

not care to have young women come out here alone and without expectancies. In Algeria, you comprehend, that has been done with very unfortunate circumstances — for the young women. And here we are taking much caution and no chances."

"Tut!" broke in the girl swiftly. "If I engage her, all is well?"

"Of a certainty. Still, as you may see, one knows little about her. It is true that she was given the Croix for her hospital work under fire. But the Croix has gone to Apaches who served *la patrie*. It might be well to wait, to cable home and inquire —"

"Nonsense!" declared Berangère calmly. "I shall engage her."

As she spoke, her eye fell upon a paper which lay on the desk of the official. She reached over and picked it up. "What is this? There is a handsome man, monsieur! *Tiens* — one thousand dollars! What has he done, then, to be worth so much to the government?"

The other shrugged. "Mademoiselle, I do not know. Me, I know nothing of it. The paper came in the official mail from Hanoi, this morning."

Berangère frowned. "An American and a criminal! This is singular."

The paper in her hand was one which bore the enlarged picture of a man — not a bad-looking fellow, excellently dressed. The face was full of possibilities. It was a bronzed and rugged face, anything but handsome from the oily and mustached French colonial standard of masculine beauty; a keen and incisive face, rather good-humored and very calm.

Beneath this picture was the name, "J. Hudson Smith. American," followed by the information that the governor general would pay one thousand piasters — locally termed dollars — for information of his whereabouts. It was an unusual thing, this circular; the police seldom follow such a system of advertising.

"I shall keep this," said Berangère coolly. "Somewhere I have seen this man; whether lately or long ago, I cannot say. But perhaps I shall gain the reward, eh?"

"Could Mademoiselle have the cruelty to deliver a poor wretch of a man to justice?"

She laughed gayly. "That remains to be seen! He must first be found."

Returning to her hotel, Berangère laid the circular upon her table and forgot it temporarily. In the course of the afternoon, Félice Bonnard appeared, was promptly engaged, and was given enough money to supply herself with a modest wardrobe. Berangère dined out, and attended a band concert in the Jardin Botanique, followed by an evening with friends.

When she finally returned home, she noted that the circular about Hudson Smith was gone. Since it was nowhere about the rooms, she concluded that it had been thrown out with the trash and so passed the matter by.

FÉLICE BONNARD was inhabiting a none too pleasant *chambre meublée* in the Rue Turc. That same evening, she left her room exactly at eight, and was joined outside by a man who had been awaiting her. They walked several blocks without speaking, came at length to the Café de la Terrasse, and took one of the outside tables beneath the tamarind trees.

When the waiter had departed with their orders, the man, who revealed himself as a well-dressed person with a rather broad, powerful face crowned by a thatch of reddish hair and adorned by a sprouting red mustache, looked at Félice and smiled.

"Well, dear sister? You succeeded?"

"Perfectly," answered Félice coolly. "I am engaged."

The other nodded. "Of course. Who could resist you?"

"You have managed it very well." Félice regarded him with a flash of cold challenge.

"Ah!" said the man blandly. "But I resist all women, my dear sister —"

"Abandon that term!" she exclaimed with a trace of anger. "I am not your sister, Paul! I do not wish you to speak again in that manner!"

The man laughed amusedly. "Very well, my dear Félice. As you wish."

The waiter arrived with their orders, and departed.

"Here is something of interest." Félice took a folded paper from her handbag. "It was lying on the table in the apartment of mademoiselle, so I brought it. The face, you understand, was interesting. Our friend M. Smith seems to be in some demand, and in case you desire to make a thousand dollars at once —"
She concluded with a shrug.

Her companion studied the handbill, then pocketed it.

"I must thank you, Félice, for this thoughtful act. We must leave town immediately."

"Then you do not want to turn him in?"

Lebrun made a gesture of dismissal. "For a thousand? Bah! We are playing for ten thousand, for a hundred thousand! He is a good man; we need him. It does not matter about your mademoiselle. If she saw this picture, she may recognize Smith on the island. But what of that?"

"When are you leaving?" asked Félice.

"Tonight," said M. le Diable, reflectively. "Le Morpion, who is a sailor and who perfectly understands navigation, will remain to bring you and Mademoiselle to the island."

"But she has a man — an old Breton —"

"Oh!" Lebrun laughed softly. "You mean, she *had* such a one! He was attended to this evening. L'Etoile and Curel tied an anchor to his neck and dropped him over the rail. Trust Le Morpion for the rest, my dear. He is very capable, that one! So is this Curel, also a seaman."

"You intend to work swiftly or slowly, Paul?"

"Slowly, of course. Who knows what may turn up? There on the island we are safe. There is none to interfere. Why not take our time? This is a case where art is worth more than brute force. Listen!"

Enthusiasm kindled in the broad, powerful features. One saw that those features held not so much a lack of refinement, as a loss of pristine refinement; as though some elder fires of evil had burned out much of the inner man, purging him of conscience and all spiritual things.

"My dear Félice, that island was absolutely made for us; the ensemble is perfect — perfect! No communication with anywhere. A fool of a fat man and his silly butterfly of a daughter. A house filled with artistic, fictitious treasures. A cellar filled with real, factitious treasure; liquor, you comprehend — the most absolute treasure in the world of today. Do you realize that America has ceased to ship liquor to us, that lack of space forbids much being sent from England and France? A cellar filled with liquors can be taken to any port on the mainland and sold instantly, where a cellar filled with gold would only excite queries. You see? Besides, there is the place itself — a magnificent health resort for one so lately undermined by hard work on Noumea, not to mention a difficult escape."

F ÉLICE regarded him with a slight frown. "You mistake," she said slowly, "when you speak of the girl as a silly butterfly. Here, I grant, she is gay and reckless and merry. But be careful! I think this girl is no fool."

M. le Diable nodded soberly. "I respect your judgment, Félice. I shall not forget it."

"Besides, what do you plan for her?"

A sardonic smile tipped his lips as he regarded her. "Ah, you look upon her with jealous eyes? Nonsense! When have you known me to look upon a woman? Never — unless it were you; and sometimes I think that even here I made a mistake."

She trembled slightly, but her eyes did not waver. "Then, about this girl — "

"Bah! I shall give her as a reward to L'Etoile. Now, by all means neglect no details; remember, I plan to remain on that island for some time. Recuperated, refreshed, enriched, we shall leave there when we wish. Then the world lies before us!"

"Before — who?" asked Félice.

"Before — well, before us two! Is that satisfactory? To your health, Veuve Bonnard! You and I, we shall spend our honeymoon in Japan!"

The woman's eyes flashed with a singular fire — a fire, one would say, of exultation. She seized and lifted her glass.

"Good! It is a promise, Paul?"

"It is a promise," the man nodded. "My promises are never broken."

His glittering black eyes watched her, a terrible gleam in their depths, as she drank; when her gaze returned to him, the gleam was gone.

A man who sat at the adjoining table, and whose eyes had several times fallen upon the face of M. le Diable, rose and departed. He strode along to the Rue Lagrandière, turned down to the middle of the block, and entered the Gendarmerie.

This man came to an office where a light showed, and entered. Inside, he found another man, like himself clad in civilian clothes, who glanced up and nodded from a paper-littered desk.

"Do you remember," said the new arrival abruptly, "a man who was brought to Hanoi from our settlement in Shanghai — a man wanted for a particularly atrocious murder in Hué City?"

"Paul Adran, alias Lebrun, alias Thomson, alias le Diable — alias everything!" said the man at the desk, without hesitation. "Suspected of being an Englishman or American. He was sentenced to Noumea for life; sentence approved by Des Gachons and appeal denied. He was transported. Well?"

"I thought tonight," said the newcomer reflectively, "that I saw him sitting at a table of the Café de la Terrasse. I only saw M. le Diable once, so I am not certain, yet —"

The other smiled. "My dear fellow, absolutely impossible!"

"All the same, let us have the Noumea report that came in two days ago."

Ten minutes later, the man at the desk read aloud a sentence.

"Drowned in attempting escape," he said. "I trust this satisfies you?"

"Evidently." The bearded one sighed. "Evidently! What about this American, this man Smith? The information that he was believed to be here in Saigon —"

"Was correct." The man at the desk glanced up, nodded. "I found this afternoon that he had been here, had been employed as a laborer at the quay."

"Had been?"

"He vanished from sight two days ago."

The newcomer made a gesture of resignation. "Not just Smith has vanished, then, but a thousand dollars, which is more to the point." He picked up several official cables and telegrams, and began to open them. "Ah!" His voice again drew the eyes of the man at the desk. "Here is word from Hanoi! We must look out for two men, known as L'Etoile and Le Morpion — descriptions given. Also a request from the governor-general himself that we leave nothing undone to locate the man Smith. Devil take it! Who is this American, and what has he done? Why do they send us no details?"

The other man shrugged his shoulders.

"Who knows? But we may find him. Five of our best men are going over the lower end of the city at this hour. What about the two who are wanted?"

"A murder and robbery in Hanoi. See that the bulletins are copied and posted in the hall at once. With luck, we may pick up all three before dawn."

At this precise moment, the men under discussion were engaged in getting supplies aboard a whaleboat which lay at the wharf, not a hundred yards from the Customs house.

CHAPTER IV

When a Star Falls a Soul Has Passed

LEBRUN had taken in charge the whaleboat, which was moored openly at the Messageries wharf on the river. Presumably, the palm of the quay watchman had been gilded, to prevent interference.

Curel and Smith were handing down provisions and boxes, while in the boat L'Etoile and Le Morpion stowed them away. Smith had known M. le Diable twenty-four hours, yet he had not the least idea of where they were going or what they were going to do. If his companions knew, they said nothing to him. Smith had not shared in the removal of Paul, the Breton boatman, but Curel had participated in that murder, with his usual bored air.

Suddenly, an indistinct figure appeared from the shadows of the godowns, darted forward and engaged in a low conversation with Lebrun. The figure darted away and was gone again. Lebrun came to the boat and spoke, addressing the two men below.

"Messieurs! The police are looking for you gentlemen. Le Morpion, you will have to go with us instead of remaining here."

There was a sound of hearty oaths from below. Monsieur the Devil took the arm of Curel and drew him to one side. He spoke in a low tone.

"You told me that you had been in the navy. You can navigate?"

"Perfectly," said Curel. "That is, if I have opium.

My pills are gone, and I can find only pipe outfits —"

"I know, I know," said Lebrun impatiently. "You who eat, cannot smoke, eh? Very well; I have a supply of pills ready for you. You must remain and take charge of that Des Gachons boat — apply for the job. Félice will make things easy for you, if you tell a convincing lie. If you cannot do it, then the devil take you! I want no inefficient ones."

"Oh, I'm scoundrel enough for anything," said Curel philosophically.

"You had better be," said Lebrun dryly. "We must get out of here at once. M. Smith! The police are in search of you!"

Smith chuckled as he joined them. "Not for the first time. I like this way of leaving town, too — right under the noses of the customs people, from the biggest wharf in the city!"

"Always audacity," quoted Lebrun, with a soft laugh and a glance at the lights of the nearby Customs house. "Everything is stowed? Very well. We must get down the river and be off Cap St. Jacques before daylight. Curel, can you accomplish your share?"

"If I have the opium."

Lebrun handed him a package. "Then, au revoir, and the devil's luck! Down with you, Smith, we're off this instant!"

SMITH climbed down into the boat; its mast was already stepped. He joined L'Etoile. Behind them sat Le Morpion. Monsieur the Devil came down, cast off the lines, and took his position in the stern at the tiller.

"Up with the sail, once we are in the tide," he ordered softly. "Watch for police boats!"

The craft floated silently out into the current of the river. It merged into the mists that writhed slowly about the surface of the muddy water, and then it was gone into the night, absorbed. Curel gazed after it for a little, then turned and walked away, tearing at the package of opium with fumbling fingers. A queer smile was set upon his dissipated face, the smile of one who sees in prospect some very singular events.

The four men in the whaleboat went down the river without hindrance. Lebrun conned the lights and steered their course; once they passed within thirty feet of a gay Fluviales steamer, whose bright lights flooded them with brilliancy. Lebrun waved ironically at those who lined the rail, as the searchlight touched him.

It seemed to occur to none of the four that they were doing a remarkable thing in thus setting out to sea in a whaleboat, bound on an errand which could hardly be philanthropic in nature. Perhaps Curel, who so hated facts, regretted that he was not with them in this mad fantasy.

When dawn heaved up out of the ocean, the whaleboat was skimming along beneath a brisk wind. The river and its narrow, widening entrance had fallen behind. To the east was a faint blur upon the horizon — Cap St. Jacques.

Lebrun headed the boat into the south, steering by a compass which lay beside him. This remarkable man was not questioned by his companions as to his navigating ability; one takes for granted that M. le Diable can do anything.

A little afterward, the four breakfasted. Then Lebrun gave over the tiller to Le Morpion, who crouched above it like a bulging-jawed dog, and lay down to sleep upon some canvas. As he stretched out, he glanced at Smith and put one hand into his pocket.

"Here is something that may interest you," he said, and handed Smith the folded paper which he had received from Félice, and which Félice Bonnard had taken from the table in the room of Berangère des Gachons. Then he closed his eyes and slept.

Smith, sitting beside L'Etoile, glanced at the paper and smiled sardonically. He took out his pipe and lighted it. Certainly, he reflected, this picture of J. Hudson Smith, shaven and trimmed and collared, looked very unlike the Smith who he was now — the dirty-jawed ruffian bound for he knew not where!

THE paper fell from his hand as he puffed. L'Etoile bent over, caught it as it fluttered. He saw the picture, and his one blazing eye opened wide in astonishment as he read at a glance the heavy lines of type below.

"Name of a dog!" he ejaculated softly, lifting his eye to Smith. "This — why, this *ventre-bleu* looks like you!"

Smith laughed. "Thank you, my friend. Looks are not deceiving."

L'Etoile started. "You — why, it's not possible! I know who this man Smith is — at least, I heard in Hanoi that he —"

Here, all in an instant, Smith perceived disaster leaping at him. His face hardened.

"You don't know everything!" he said in a low voice. "Be careful!"

L'Etoile was so utterly taken aback by astonishment, that for an instant he could only stare, incredulous.

"But — why, I never connected you with *him!* This dog of hell is the one who —"

Smith's fingers gripped his arm.

"Be careful!" said Smith quietly. He realized that Le Morpion, who could hear nothing of what they said, was gazing at them curiously. "Be careful, I warn you!"

From L'Etoile broke a sudden bursting snarl of fury.

"You — hell be kind to you!" he gasped. "So this is your game, is it —"

The hand of Smith tightened on his arm. But the other arm moved, flashed, drove in and out like the head of a striking snake.

The other hand of Smith was in his jacket pocket. That pocket vomited a splash of red flame, gave vent to a single smashing report. From Le Morpion came a hoarse, inarticulate bellow. The figure of Lebrun leaped straight upright, pistol in hand. But there was no need. L'Etoile had fallen back against the corner of thwart and gunnel. His two hands were clasped about his throat, and through the fingers seeped a dreadful tide of bubbling crimson. A knife had fallen from his fingers into his lap. His one blazing eye stared for a moment at Lebrun, his lips were open and vainly trying to utter a word. Then his lips closed, his one eye fluttered shut, and he fell back in limp death.

Smith sat motionless, his left hand bringing a pistol into sight. Over his face was creeping a deathly pallor. His eyes went to Lebrun.

"What's this?" crackled the latter's voice.

"We disagreed," said Smith. "You've lost L'Etoile. Don't ask questions, you fool! You'll lose me if you don't give me — a hand — quick!"

His right hand, pressed against his side, came away red. L'Etoile's knife had bitten him. Then, quietly, he laid down the pistol and doubled forward, unconscious.

"He shot L'Etoile!" cried out Le Morpion, his voice terrible. One would have said that this scoundrel, this unspeakable ruffian, was pierced by grief for his dead comrade in sin. "He shot L'Etoile —"

Lebrun gestured for silence.

"Don't be a fool, you! What caused the quarrel?"

"I couldn't hear. They were talking. L'Etoile snapped with his knife —"

"And paid for it," said Lebrun. "I am sorry. But this fellow Smith — did you note how he used his brains? Said I'd lose him if I didn't act! Clever, I call it. He knew that I couldn't afford to lose two at once. Keep your hands off him, understand? This man is worth a hundred. He has more brains than L'Etoile."

"How about me?" grunted Le Morpion.

"You're a friend. He's a mercenary. Besides, he is to be blamed for our future sins."

Le Morpion saw sense in this, and said no more, although his eyes were very dark and evil.

MEANTIME, Lebrun was bending over the figure of Smith. Removing jacket and shirt, he laid bare the side — white, firm skin marred by an ugly gash that welled slow blood. Then, and coolly enough, Lebrun searched the unconscious man from hair to sox; searched him thoroughly, carefully, unhurriedly. Whatever the object of his search, it was unattained. He replaced everything.

After this, he gave his attention to the wound, which was not serious. He bound it very deftly, re-placed shirt and jacket, and left Smith to recover of his own volition. He picked up the body of L'Etoile, poised it a moment at the boat's edge, and sent it over-board.

"A good friend, a faithful friend, an honest friend!" he said, gazing out after the bobbing speck. Yet, perhaps, the words were sardonic; there was a queer gleam in his black eyes as he gazed.

"What brought it on?" demanded Le Morpion sulkily. "What caused it?"

Monsieur the Devil shook his head.

"Who knows? Waken me when this man opens his eyes. Touch him not. Speak not. Only — waken me."

With this, he took his former place on the canvas, and appeared to fall asleep at once.

The morning wore past in magnificence of soli-tude, the sun blazing in the sky, the ocean all blue-green and desolate, empty of ships. The whaleboat skimmed on and on, pushed steadily by the crisp breeze, Le Morpion steering her skillfully and cunningly. Once or twice, when his eyes wandered to the inert figure of Smith, the sail wavered, for he was steering by the wind rather than by compass. The seas swung past endlessly, the foam hissing and swirling under the lee rail to bubble out behind in a thin wake. On the canvas, Lebrun slept, an arm over his face; above the tiller crouched Le Morpion, watching, always watching.

Then, suddenly, the eyes of Smith opened.

Le Morpion was gazing upward at the moment. Like the Indian who does not see the waving grass yet perceives something amiss with Nature's ordering, this man perceived the movement. An inarticulate word came from his lips. Instantly, Lebrun sat up and gazed at Smith; he was wide awake, speaking, even as he sat up. One would have thought that he had slept with the words breaking on his lips, so swiftly did he speak.

"Ah! Smith, what did you and L'Etoile quarrel over?"

Smith, equally alert, was conscious that much time had passed since the affray. He saw danger in the question. He read danger in the intent gaze which Le Morpion bent upon him.

"Quarrel?" he responded. "I remember now — why, there was no quarrel! He drew a knife and struck; I shot him."

"Ah!" said Lebrun calmly, regarding him. "Well, let it pass. You are thirsty? There is water beside you."

No MORE WAS said. None the less, Smith was subtly aware that he had not given the right answer. He felt intuitively that he had bungled somehow; yet he was too thirsty to care. He got the water and drank. Lebrun went to sleep again.

After some time, Lebrun awakened and took the tiller while Le Morpion crawled up forward, munched some biscuit and curled up in slumber. Smith stared up at the calm gaze of Monsieur the Devil, and voiced the question that was bothering him.

"Where are we going?"

Lebrun's black eyes glittered on him reflectively.

"To an island. To a place of vengeance. There is a man whom I hate, whom I shall kill; then we take his possessions. His name, Des Gachons."

The eyes of Smith widened a trifle.

"Des Gachons!" he repeated in a low voice.

Lebrun regarded him attentively. "What? You know him?"

Smith feebly shook his head. "No. But he may know me."

"No. He has been out of official affairs for quite a long time. He will not know that you are wanted, that there is any reward for you. Nor will he know me, since he never saw me; although he might have seen my picture. We must chance that."

"I'm not worried about you," said Smith. "But when he knew me, I was employed by the government."

"Ah!" said Monsieur the Devil calmly. "This is news. In what capacity?"

Smith allowed his head to droop for an instant. He was lying now, and lying artistically; he was not so weak as he seemed. Still, there was not great strength left in him.

"If I told you, then you would consider it a lie."

"None the less," said Lebrun, regarding him, "I would advise you to tell me."

There was something deadly in these words.

"I was an engineer — of construction. With the new railroad. Not long ago, I needed money — I made a mess of things, but got away."

Lebrun nodded. "Then you got the money?"

"I have five thousand dollars in my belt."

Lebrun had discovered this money in his search. He nodded his head.

"Very well. Now go to sleep — there will be no difficulty about Des Gachons."

The matter was closed. None the less, Smith retained an uncomfortable conviction that he had somehow bungled. Not in words, perhaps, but in some detail — a glance, a gesture!

However, there was nothing to be done about it now, and he dropped off to sleep.

CHAPTER V

It Is Dangerous to Invoke the Devil

J. HUDSON SMITH, lying in the boat or sitting propped against his rolled jacket, spent several uncomfortable, painful and reflective days. His wound was developing badly; had taken on a touch of fever which made Lebrun frown over the dressings. Lebrun was a good surgeon, deft and cunning in the fingers. This man seemed a good everything.

A good navigator, certainly. He guided the whale-boat over the waste of waters without help from Le Morpion, and with unerring certitude. There were charts and instruments in the boat. During these days, Smith learned for the first time, from conversation and scattered hints, how Lebrun had come to find the island owned by Des Gachons.

The American could guess at much of the story which remained untold — much at which even M. le Diable himself seemed now to reluct in thought and word. It was an odyssey fit for the devil himself! Bad enough was the escape from that infernal paradise, Noumea; the escape, tinctured with blood and desperation, imbued with images of savage, naked brown men, of weary-eyed guards, of the night swim past the ships and that little island which sits in the jaws of the harbor and vomits the shrieks of tortured humanity. Worse yet was the sequel, the tossing for days and nights upon a crazy raft of brush, the finding of a life-buoy lost from some ship or some corpse, the savage persistency of spirit which held the failing body ever to its work. After this, the island; the last flickering effort of the iron will, and safety. Following upon these things, the flame of vengeance toward the man who had finally succeeded in sending him to the penal colony.

Smith realized that he was going to be in a bad way unless his wound quickly received antiseptic treatment; but he fought down the fever and held his peace. He had little to do but study his companions. Le Morpion possessed a good deal at bottom; a sullen brute, yet capable withal, and extremely cunning. But the other, this Monsieur the Devil — here was a man not to be fathomed or understood! Mentally abnormal beyond doubt. Somehow warped into a career of undiluted deviltry. In brief, an enemy of society.

Then, at last, the unceasing monotony of sky and sea was broken; in that long sword-like line of the horizon appeared a slight nick. This came at sunset. With dawn, the nick had grown into a green smudge, and by noon the whaleboat was off the entrance to the island harbor.

Here Lebrun delayed purposely. There was evident commotion ashore; the small cruiser taken to Saigon by Berangère had not yet returned. The whaleboat came slowly in toward the curving crescent of beach, where, in obvious agitation, Jean Marie Auguste des Gachons was marshalling his forces to receive the unexpected visitors.

The escalier was working fast; the two secretaries,

the gardener, the chef, and several native servants appeared on the beach, and Des Gachons stood at their head. Lebrun, smiling thinly, directed the boat to the sand at his very feet.

SMITH watched and listened sardonically. Was it possible that the judge would not recognize the criminal? True, Lebrun was changed now; the reddish mustache altered his entire appearance, nor was there anything of the criminal in his bearing. Quite the contrary.

"Who are you?" boomed out Des Gachons, theatrically. His pose was majestic.

Lebrun leaped out to the sand, drew in the prow of the boat, turned, and rendered an elaborate bow.

"Monsieur," he said gravely, "you see before you three shipwrecked unfortunates. I am a humble devotee of ethnology, mineralogy, and the scientific arts; Paul Lebrun by name, an unsuccessful aspirant for the Prix Goncourt in times past, and for some years a student of the sciences of China."

Before he could proceed further, Des Gachons advanced with open arms and tendered him a warm Gallic embrace. "Colleague, I welcome you!" he exclaimed sonorously. "You have come to a good house of hospitality. I, too, am something of a savant in my unworthy way; Des Gachons by name —"

"What!" exclaimed Lebrun, drawing back in astonishment. "Not the author of that admirable and learned treatise upon the ethnologic significance of the lamaic rosaries?"

"The same," admitted Des Gachons modestly.

"Then it is a kindly fate which has drawn us to your shore!" cried Lebrun. "To think that I have touched the hand of this master! I am overcome! But I forget our friends. Allow me to present to you an American gentleman, a fellow passenger on our hapless coasting steamer — Monsieur Smith. He was hurt during a wild scramble for the boats, you comp!ehend. And this is one called Le Morpion, an excellent seaman, to whose care and skill we all owe our lives."

"Ah!" said Des Gachons briskly. "A wounded man? Monsieur, have no fear! We shall care for you excellently! We have guests; that is admirable! I welcome you!"

It was at this point that Smith gave way suddenly; the overtensed nerves, the overstrained muscles, collapsed. He realized that he was burning with fever, and fell asleep. The words that had formed upon his lips remained unuttered. . . .

When he wakened, it was to find himself lying in a bed. The room about him was, to his disordered senses, a room of some eastern palace. Real furniture, real paintings on the walls, real flowers at the window! He was in a guest room, of course. What made it more terribly real, was Le Morpion sitting beside him, watching.

And Le Morpion stayed there, as though he had orders to this effect.

A day had passed, thought Smith; it was another morning, and the fever was gone out of him. He did not try to speak. He lay silent and unmoving; as he lay, there came voices from outside the open window, which in fact overlooked the sunken garden. They were the voices of Des Gachons and Lebrun.

Their host, gathered the American, was about to show Lebrun over his island estate. To this M. de Diable objected for a moment.

"One thing, dear colleague!" he protested. "I wish your opinion upon a vexed point. For some time I have been studying the question of turquoise in China — a most interesting problem!"

"Most interesting, indeed," agreed the voice of Des Gachons. "Well?"

"You are aware that the stone is unknown in many provinces of China," pursued Lebrun, proving himself master of some astonishing knowledge. "Indeed, it is regarded as pertaining to barbarians; it did not enter imperial circles until the K'ien-lung period of the Chings. It was regarded as a form of petrified or transformed fir, as is indicated by its present name of *lu sung shi* or `green fir-tree stone.' Yet we know that Marco Polo —"

"Exactly!" exclaimed Des Gachons eagerly. "He spoke of the monopoly —"

"I am coming to that. My theory is that the stone was introduced under the Mongol emperors, and that its mining and use was broken up during Ming times, not to be revived until the recent K'ien-lung period. I base this theory on the fact that the earliest word for the stone is *tien-tse*, occurring in the *Cho-keng-lu,* published in 1366. Therefore —"

The voices drifted off and became indistinct.

Smith saw Le Morpion glance at the window, a dark smile hovering about his ugly lips.

Smith saw nothing of his host. As the hours passed, native servants appeared, but Le Morpion never left the room. One would have fancied this man utterly devoted to the wounded American; but in this devotion, Smith read a sinister significance. Very possibly Le Morpion was here to guard against any delirious babbling.

The native servants of the establishment numbered three. They were a man and two women, brown creatures who spoke French after a fashion, and who had been fetched from the mainland. They were ignorant and timorous creatures, quite devoid of any graces or civilized culture; the man and his two wives had been brought here to serve, and they served — that was all. As for the polygamous aspect of the case, in these days when one can get servants at all, one does not inquire too closely into their private lives, *n'est ce pas?*

LEBRUN, on this fine morning, had terminated his argument anent turquoise, and was accompanying his host upon a walk about the place — a walk which was destined to terminate very unhappily for Jean Marie Auguste des Gachons.

This simple and honest-hearted fat man was supremely happy. To have his little paradise invaded by three unfortunates to whom he could give shelter and aid, was a pleasure. To find that one of these men was a fellow savant, a person of discernment and much ethnologic lore, was a delight. To find himself recognized as a master, deferred to, regarded with awe and honor, was a supreme happiness.

So Des Gachons accounted himself fortunate, and devoted his energies to showing Lebrun about the place. First came the house itself; a house built not for show, but for living in. The cellars were exhibited with some complacency — indeed, there was a stock of liquors in them which was now worth a small fortune alone.

The kitchen, under its French chef, an excellent man with a brain like that of an ox in all things save food. The collections in their cases — jewels and rare works of art from all the eastern coasts; an excellent array of gilded bronzes, champlevé and cloisonné from China, and some magnificent porcelains. If Des Gachons made his money in princely fashion, he had also spent it in the same way.

After the house, the exterior, with the old gardener proud of his work; the establishment was on display, and all recognized it. And at last, ignorant that his visitor knew the way no less than he, Des Gachons took Lebrun down the avenue of palms to the swimming pool.

This was now the same as when he had first looked upon it, except that there was no golden figure aflame in the sunlight. The two men circled that pool of cerulean blue, Des Gachons opened the gate in the wall, and they passed to the fantastic little orchard, with the cliff and the sea beyond.

Here Des Gachons paused, and sighed as he surveyed the place.

"This was planned for the hot days, my friend," he said, waving his hand about the orchard. "You comprehend, one visits the pool, which is fed by springs; then one comes out here beneath the trees with a book, perhaps, and sits on the cliff and watches the sea. I must set about building the little summer-house which I have planned, to perch just here on the edge of the cliff."

HE INDICATED the spot. The two men stood there at the verge, and gazed on the sparkling waters beneath. Perhaps Lebrun was thinking of how he had come here first, naked and perishing; how he had struggled up this cliff to the place where they now stood. His eyes were somber as he regarded that cliff.

"One does not miss the city here," said Des Gachons, pulling at his pronged beard and looking vastly complacent. "It was work, of course, building all this; vessels and laborers and architects, you understand. But now — it is a paradise!"

"It is indeed," said Lebrun in a low voice. "But do not forget, my friend, that into the earthly Paradise came Satan!"

Des Gachons regarded him with a smile.

"What do you mean, then?"

Lebrun took a cheroot from his pocket and lighted it, leisurely.

"I have some knowledge of which you may be ignorant," he said. "Do you remember having passed upon the sentence of a criminal who was called M. le Diable?"

Des Gachons frowned, considered, and at length uttered an exclamation.

"Ah, yes! *Tron de l'air!*" Like the immortal Tartarin, this fat man was also of the south. "M. le Diable! Of course; the man was a hardened criminal, a degenerate bit of humanity, who was caught by our people in Shanghai. He had committed atrocious murders in the province. He was said to be at the head of a band of desperate Apaches. I remember very well. It gave me tremendous satisfaction to be rid of such a person — he was sent to Noumea for life. One does not live long in Noumea, you comprehend."

"Exactly," said Lebrun in a dry tone.

"It was most unfortunate," reflected Des Gachons, "that this man alone was taken, and not all the members of his gang. I remember recommending most urgently to my successor that no pains be spared to hunt down and root out every branch of this evil tree! But, my friend, what caused you to bring this criminal to memory?"

"Because," said Lebrun, "I heard recently that he had escaped from Noumea."

Des Gachons started. His ruddy countenance blanched slightly.

"Impossible! No man can escape from Noumea; one dies there, but escapes — never!"

"No man, perhaps," said Lebrun calmly. "But Monsieur the Devil — that is another matter entirely! However, there are two versions of the story. One that he escaped; another, that he died in Noumea and came to life elsewhere. Are you interested in hearing them?"

Des Gachons stared at him. "But — but — you are saying incredible things!"

"Incredible? Nothing is incredible, when one believes in a personal devil!" returned Lebrun. His smile was, as the French say, *"sourd"* — a coldly disdainful, inexpressible smile. "One story goes that he escaped by sea, and that the sea brought him to this island."

Des Gachons started again, this time more violently. From his pallid lips was wrung a low cry.

"This — this is some jest, monsieur?"

"On the contrary, unfortunately," said Lebrun. "The story says this criminal came here, stole one of your boats, and departed."

"The whaleboat!" cried Des Gachons. "The whaleboat that was missing!"

"Exactly. This M. le Diable took your boat and departed. He went to the mainland, found the remnants of his old gang, and planned a *razzia* upon your island. Probably he did not regard you with any feeling of gratitude —"

Des Gachons staggered, his face pale as the dead. "Incredible! This — this is some frightful lie —"

"Possibly." Lebrun made a calm gesture of assent. "The other story runs that he died in Noumea. Well, he died — and he came to life again later. You understand? The devil could hardly die, my dear monsieur; at least, the life after death of M. le Diable would be most fascinating to contemplate, from the stand-point of science, is it not? Still, in either case we arrive at the same conclusions; namely, that he would come to interview you —"

"Devil fly away with me!" ejaculated the other, thickly.

"Precisely." Lebrun bowed. "I am M. le Diable, at your service. Let us fly, by all means!"

He threw away his cheroot and approached Des Gachons, upon his lips a terrible smile.

CHAPTER VI

Queer Things Occur in the Kitchen

SMITH and Le Morpion were alone in the room, shortly after noon, when Lebrun joined them. M. le Diable took a chair beside the bed and inquired with solicitude after the patient.

"I'm all right," said Smith. "A bit weak, naturally."

Lebrun nodded. "Very good! You are hungry?"

"Somewhat. What's the matter with luncheon?"

"Nothing; I have just come from the kitchen, and I assure you that an excellent meal is waiting. A very excellent meal, in fact!"

The trifling detail that Lebrun had just come from the kitchen, quite escaped the attention of J. Hudson Smith at the instant. Before he could respond, the figure of one of the secretaries appeared in the doorway.

"Ah, M. Lebrun! Your pardon — the chef told me that you had returned — luncheon is served, monsieur! Can you inform us where M. des Gachons has vanished to?"

Lebrun smiled. "I can, monsieur. He is at this moment located near the cliff beyond the swimming pool, and is contemplating a serious poem upon immortality, after the manner of M. Ronsard. He requests that luncheon go forward without awaiting his coming; as for myself, I shall remain here to watch the condition of my patient, if you will be good enough to send me something on a tray. Le Morpion, do you wish to be relieved?"

Lebrun turned as he asked the question. Perhaps he made an imperceptible sigh; at all events, Le Morpion shook his sullen head.

"I remain also," he said.

"Very well, messieurs," said the secretary respectfully, and vanished. Lebrun rose and shut the door. Then he bowed mockingly toward it, and turned, a thin smile upon his lips.

"This poem upon which our host is working," he said, "will be a famous thing, I assure you! The only trouble is that it will never be finished."

Le Morpion looked up suddenly, a queer gleam in his eyes.

" 'Cre nom!" he ejaculated. "Then — you have struck?"

"I have struck," said Lebrun, his voice somber. "I have struck — from top to bottom!"

A peculiar exultation appeared in his broad, powerful features; a singular look of mingled ferocity, exhilaration, and gloomy satisfaction. Smith half raised himself upon one elbow.

"You —" He paused, wetting his lips. "You mean —"

"I am avenged," said Monsieur the Devil. "Des Gachons, standing at the verge of a cliff, became ambitious to emulate Daedalus in flight. Well, he flew! But as he had neither the wings of Daedalus, nor the faith of Saint Peter, he could neither remain in the air nor upon the sea. In fact, the devil flew away with him!"

Lebrun turned. "Le Morpion, there is one whom you must handle: the gardener. He is now at work in the garden. He does not eat in the middle of the day; hence, I assign him to you!"

Le Morpion nodded and rose. He made a curt gesture, and strode from the room.

SMITH sank back upon his bed, his hands clenched beneath the covers. Des Gachons — dead! The thing was incredible, fearful beyond words! There had been no chance to give warning.

"M. American," said Lebrun, standing beside the bed and regarding Smith attentively, "you appear overcome by this news!"

"I am," said Smith steadily. He looked up into the glittering black eyes; they smiled down at him almost frostily.

"Well, you understand that with me everyone must earn his keep? You have done nothing; you can do nothing, at least for a day or two. Therefore, your value to me must lie only in the future. I have decided what to do with you."

It occurred to Smith that he was to be murdered immediately. "Yes?" he drawled. "May I be pardoned a touch of curiosity, then?"

Lebrun chuckled. "I have decided to give you a wife."

"Ah! There is an Eve in this Garden of Eden?"

"There will be," said Lebrun, "by tonight; or so I calculate. Curel should arrive tonight beyond question. You shall have a wife; *une vierge charmante,* and you shall console her for the loss of her father. This will, of course, be besides the division of the spoils."

He made a gesture, and turned away.

Smith lay with his eyes closed, not daring to speak, lest he disclose a more agile brain than Lebrun gave him credit for. He perceived clearly that he had been picked to bear the brunt of this entire adventure. Lebrun, perhaps, did not wish the death of Berangère des Gachons; he planned to bestow this human spoil upon Smith, whom he already knew to be badly wanted by the authorities. Then he would see to it that Smith was apprehended — a scapegoat.

It was an excellent plan. The only flaw in it was that Smith was not exactly the person whom Lebrun supposed him to be.

THE door opened. One of the native servants entered, bearing a tray. This tray was set upon a rolling table, and the table brought to the bedside. The servant placed a chair for Lebrun, who nodded, and then left the room.

"Go with my blessing to what awaits you!" murmured M. le Diable. Then, bending above the tray, he uttered an exclamation of satisfaction. "Ah, an admirable chef! Here we have *bondons au lait, beignets aromatisés* — above all, excellent curried rice. Superb, this rice!"

From the tray, Lebrun picked the last-named dish, the *pièce de résistance* of the luncheon. Removing the large silver cover, Lebrun lifted this dish and carried it to the window. There he paused, looking out into the garden. Smith watched his actions in puzzled wonder.

"Does it occur to you," reflected Lebrun aloud,

"that M. des Gachons populated this island with birds? A charming touch of sentiment! Yet it is inevitable that when the master falls, the entire establishment falls with him."

So saying, he hurled the dish through the open window.

For an instant it seemed to the American that this man must have gone mad. No other explanation of this astounding conduct came to him. Without comment, Lebrun returned to his place and sat down, pouring the wine.

"I believe there is enough remaining for us all," he observed. "Come, my dear Smith! You have a very romantic name. Would it be indelicate in me to hint that it might be assumed?"

Smith grinned faintly and took the glass of wine handed him. The port brought swift color into his cheeks.

"It's my own name, all right," he returned, forcing himself to ignore that he sat face to face with the murderer of Des Gachons. "That's more than you can say, eh?"

"TOUCHÉ! A fair hit." Lebrun chuckled. "Eat, and grow strong! I'll have need of your muscles in a week or so. We shall want to have everything loaded up aboard that big motor cruiser down below, in case any unexpected thing turns up and makes us run for it. With this work done, we shall compose ourselves, unworried. So, eat!"

Smith obeyed the order, in silence. The frightful

sang-froid of this man was threatening to unnerve him, and he knew that he must struggle against such an event. He himself was helpless to act in any capacity; whatever befell, he could do nothing — yet.

It had been his intention to warn Des Gachons at all costs; he had never imagined that Lebrun would strike so swiftly and terribly. The knife of L'Etoile had been a far better friend to him than Lebrun dreamed!

The thought of Berangère des Gachons appalled the American with its possibilities. He had picked up enough by this time to know why Curel had stayed behind; yet, strangely enough, the thought of Curel gave him hope. This man, at least, was not the devil Lebrun had proved!

IN THE midst of these reflections he heard a staggering step outside the door. The door opened, and Le Morpion came into the room — came into the room and halted, swaying a little as he stood, one hand pressed against his thigh.

"Well, master," he said gruffly, "it is done."

Lebrun sprang to his feet. "What? You are hurt?"

Le Morpion, smiling grimly, removed the hand from his thigh, to betray a rush of crimson.

"Not hurt," he responded, "but a trifle nicked. The fool tried to prune me with his shears, and got a fair start before I wrung his neck. Work for you, master!"

He half fell into the chair that Lebrun shoved at him, and began to bare his thigh.

So, the gardener murdered! How far did Lebrun

mean to carry this infernal work? A cold horror gripped upon the American as he watched the scene.

M. le Diable fell to work upon the wound — a rather bad gash across the hip. It would have to be sutured; bidding the imperturbable Le Morpion hold the wound and await his return, Lebrun rose and vanished hastily from the room.

He had been gone only a short while, when from somewhere within the house cracked the burst of a pistol-shot, followed by silence. Le Morpion quivered slightly, tried to rise, then fell back with a groan. Suddenly in the doorway appeared M. le Diable. In one hand he bore a violin, in the other a gaily embroidered workbag.

"The shot!" growled Le Morpion, staring at him. "What was it?"

"Nothing," said Lebrun calmly. "One of the secretaries, poor fellow, realized that he was at the point of death, and tried to kill me. He was dying as he fired; the bullet missed. Come, we shall take a needle from the bag, a string from the violin — and tomorrow you will be limping briskly around."

He suited his actions to the words, and having selected a needle, cut a gut string from the violin. From Le Morpion broke an astonished oath.

"Dead! Then what have you done?"

Lebrun looked up from his task and smiled.

"I? Nothing. I visited the kitchen, that is all. If you will go to the window, you will see a little circle of dead birds. Well, I threw out this window our dish of curried rice, and the birds ate it. As for that downstairs, the entire household declared it excellent, I have no doubt. But when arsenic works, it works swiftly."

"What?" cried Le Morpion admiringly. "You managed them all?"

"All but the gardener," said Lebrun with a gesture of deprecation. "We shall have no need of the gardener. Neither shall we have need of secretaries. As for the chef, I am sure that the Veuve Bonnard is a superb cook. As for the servants — well, we must make shift to serve ourselves! After all, it will not be a hardship; this house is excellently stocked with all we shall require."

"Then," said Le Morpion, "we are alone on the premises?"

"We are alone," and Lebrun smiled. "Come, your leg!"

J. HUDSON SMITH lay with his eyes closed, his face white as death, a light sweat beading his brow. Swift and ruthless as lightning, M. le Diable had struck.

How long he lay, thus, Smith did not know. When at length he opened his eyes, he was alone in the room, and the door was closed. Once certain of this, he managed to sit up in bed, at the cost of a little pain. The fever was gone.

Beside the bed still stood the table bearing the luncheon tray. There was some wine left in the bottle; Smith drank it, and felt strength flood into his veins — fictitious strength, but none the less strength! He put aside the covers, swung his feet to the floor, and rose.

He swayed for a moment, until the drawn muscles about his hurt side reacted. As he waited, thus, it came to him that he had need of caution. What was done, was done; Lebrun had made a clean sweep of everyone on the island, it appeared. No use thinking of the past! Better to dismiss it and plan for the future.

Smith stepped out, and found himself not so weak as he had supposed. Near at hand was a closet. He opened the door, and found his clothes hung there carefully — all intact, even to his money belt. There was but one thing missing; and this was the one thing in search of which Smith had come — his automatic.

He turned away, his lips sternly set. With some difficulty he crossed to a dresser, near the door of a tiled bathroom. Here he paused and glanced into the mirror. A cry came to his lips at sight of the face which greeted him — bearded, gaunt, unfamiliar! Then he remembered that he had not shaved since leaving Saigon.

Turning into the bathroom, he saw a cabinet at hand bearing all that he desired, and without hesitation he seized a shaving brush and set to work.

Half an hour later, he staggered back to bed and crawled under the covers, exhausted but feeling like a new man. He was asleep almost on the instant, and he did not waken until, some hours later, a laugh aroused him. He looked up to see Lebrun standing beside him smiling.

"Well, old man, you look like a gentleman!" exclaimed Lebrun. "I see you've been busily engaged. A cigar?" He extended an excellent cheroot, which Smith accepted gladly, and held a match.

"How is Le Morpion?"

"Oh, in a bad temper — nothing worse." Lebrun waved his hand. "He'll be walking by the morning. I tell you I've been working this afternoon! Real work."

Smith could guess what manner of work this had been, but he repressed the shiver that came upon him.

"Yes?" he inquired calmly. "By the way, how shall you account to Mlle. des Gachons for the absence of so many people? Or shall you endeavor to account at all?"

"But certainly!" exclaimed M. le Diable, laughing softly. "I have already prepared a letter written in the exact hand of Des Gachons himself, informing her that ptomaine poisoning is responsible for the deplorable lack of human life here; this letter was written by a dying man, you see? We arrived in time to bury everyone. It has been neatly done, I assure you. She will not suspect — at least, for some time. When the crisis comes, then we may have to use a show of force. Well, you must excuse me now; I brought a book or two from the library for you."

He indicated several volumes on a chair by the bed, and departed. Smith gazed after him with a frown of vain wonder; he could not understand this man in the least.

"I don't want to understand him, either," he relected, taking one of the books. "Still, I'd like to know if it was he who removed my pistol!"

The house was silent and deserted. Smith read; forced himself to read, in order that his brain might be distracted from too much contemplation. Some time later, his lids drooped and he fell asleep over his book.

When he was aroused, the room was in darkness. He was wide awake instantly, with the uneasy sense that there was a strange presence in the room. He heard someone stumble and kick aside a chair; there came an oath in a voice that certainly was not that of either Lebrun or Le Morpion. Smith waited, silent.

A match flamed, and a candle sprang into quick fire as though still hot from having been recently extinguished. Smith looked up to see a figure beside him bearing a tray. It was the figure of Curel.

"You!" he exclaimed in astonishment. "Ah — then you have come!"

"We have come," said Curel in a mournful voice. "And here is your supper and mine; not much, heaven knows, but enough! The others are dining downstairs."

"The others?"

"Mme. Bonnard, our sister in complicity, and M. le Diable. Mademoiselle has gone to her room. She is, I think, somewhat overcome by grief. Damn Lebrun! If I had foreseen what was about to happen here, if I had known that girl —"

"Well?" said Smith, as the other put down the tray and paused. "What would you have done?"

Curel laughed harshly. "I would have come all the same, very likely! Well, it is a droll world; but here is some very fine Sauterne. Your health, monsieur!"

Curel poured himself a glass of wine and gulped it, as though in need of the stimulant.

CHAPTER VII

A Woman Has Her Own Ideas

AT THIS moment Smith was struck by a singular fact. He knew very well that those who are addicted to opium, usually shun liquor, which seems to kill the deadening effect of the drug. Yet Curel, who was a gentleman by birth, did not drink his Sauterne as either a gentleman or an opium addict should. On the contrary, he gulped it avidly, as though seeking in it a stimulant and cordial. Curel had the manner of one who has just been profoundly shocked and horrified.

"My dear M. Smith," he said, leaning back and surveying Smith, "I feel some pity for you."

"Thanks," said the American. "Why?"

"You perceive the result of yourself from extinguishing L'Etoile. Now, it will be even more difficult to do away with Le Morpion; who, I assure you, can bite worse than his namesake! Still worse, I am convinced, will prove the Veuve Bonnard. After all this, you will be stabbed, shot, backbroken — yet there will remain the worst of all, M. le Diable himself —"

"What are you driving at?" demanded Smith, raising himself to one elbow and regarding Curel from narrowed lids. "Do you think I'm an assassin?"

"By no means, dear comrade! However, I am a philosopher; I view what passes with an air of abstraction — usually. But now it is different. Now I am about to make you a proposal."

"Make it," said Smith curtly, wondering what the man was coming to.

"It is this: that you take care of Le Morpion and Félice, since I cannot touch a woman. I will undertake to remove Monsieur."

Smith started. "What? You mean that you would join me —"

Curel rose to his feet and yawned.

"You wonder, perhaps?" he said. "Well, there is an explanation. I am not the same poor devil whom you saw in Saigon. You comprehend I have spent some time in the company of Mlle. Berangère! I take for granted that you will not scruple to betray the devil in order to save an angel — particularly when you have become acquainted with the angel! Moreover, as I hinted in Saigon, I am somewhat acquainted with your past; hence I can guess at certain things in the present. Think over my proposal until tomorrow. *Au revoir!*"

So saying, Curel hastily left the room, disregarding the meal he had brought.

DURING the remainder of the evening Smith was left to his own devices, not a little to his relief. He found it exceedingly hard to digest the proposal of Curel; he was both amazed and suspicious.

Suspicion, however, was scarcely justified — he realized this quickly enough. Here was a man who still retained something of the gentleman; coming in contact with Lebrun and what Lebrun had done, he instinctively revolted. Curel, or De Curel, must have been in ignorance of all that was intended. Certainly, he had been terribly upset upon getting here. News of the supposed ptomaine poisoning must have been broken to Berangère rather ungently; at all events, the shock had been no less severe to Curel than to the girl.

The amazement of Smith was more justified than was his first impulse to suspicion. This offer of alliance was the last thing he expected. There was some reason for thinking that Curel would be neutral — but an active aid! This was different. It was distinctly encouraging. And yet —

What about this girl, Berangère?

"I'll have to go slow until I can see her," thought Smith. "If she's some little fool, some hysterical feminine doll, I'd better put her in the motor boat and beat it. If not — well, let the future manage itself! Curel was right about my chances of surviving, however; I'd better lose no time, or Le Morpion won't be easy to handle."

So thinking, he fell asleep.

IN THE morning, his breakfast was brought by Félice Bonnard. It was not his first sight of this extraordinary person; he had met her, briefly, in Saigon. When she had arranged the tray, she stepped back and surveyed him in silence. Her air was saturnine, unsmiling.

"You have changed," she announced critically. "And for the better. I understand that you have undertaken to tame my mistress?"

In the last word was a covert sneer — a flash of the eye, a twist of the lip.

"That, I believe," responded Smith calmly, "is the arrangement. Do you object?"

She shrugged. Already, without word or reason, there had risen between them a wall of intense dislike. On the part of Félice, this feeling was tinctured with lofty contempt. "You are not the man for the job," was her cool response. "But since it is settled — take warning! The girl is no fool."

"Ah!" The American's brows were elevated. "Yet she engaged you?"

"Take care, you!" she retorted, a slow flush mantling her cheek. "A word from me, and the master will put you out — pouf! — like a candle."

SMITH regarded her with a cold smile. Already he perceived how one of his difficulties might be removed. He could scarcely kill a woman, and this was a woman who would require killing — nothing less. A woman? No; a snake. Yet she was no more than a sharer in the crimes of Lebrun; thus far, she had done nothing overt. To kill her would be difficult.

"The master?" he replied slowly. "I suppose you mean *your* master, charming Félice! Are you not capable, then, of extinguishing your own candles?"

Her eyes hardened beneath this raillery; her face became harsh, livid.

"You are impudent to me — you!" she said in a level voice. "Take care!"

"If you have finished your warnings," said Smith, with a gesture of dismissal, "you may go. I require nothing further, thank you."

She darted him one glance that was barbed with venom, then swept from the room.

The breakfast was excellent, and Smith enjoyed it to the full. When he had finished, he rose, made shift to bathe, and dressed. There were clothes laid out for him — garments of silk; but he revolted at wearing the clothes of murdered men, and he got into his own frayed attire. This effort left him nearly exhausted. He reached an old fashioned bell-pull near the door, dragged at the cord, and sank into a chair.

In response to this summons, Curel appeared.

"*Tiens!* Up and dressed? But —"

"Some coffee, Curel," broke in the American. "I need it. And an automatic."

Curel nodded, caught up the tray, and vanished. In ten minutes he reappeared, bearing a cup of hot coffee. With this, he set down an automatic pistol.

"I trust," he observed whimsically, as Smith pocketed the weapon and gulped the coffee, "that you anticipate no executions this morning?"

"Don't be a fool." Smith chuckled. "Get me a stick, will you? A cane. Help me to reach the garden, bring me something to read, and leave me to recuperate by myself."

"Willingly."

In twenty minutes, Smith was seated in an easy chair in the sunken garden, drinking in the warm sunlight and the perfume of the trees around. Magazines and cheroots were nearby. Curel had departed.

As he sat here, Smith was oppressed by the sudden loneliness of this beautiful place. As if by the touch of a malignant hand, all those who lived here had been swept away. Everything was yet eloquent of them; the personality of Des Gachons lingered in the place he had loved.

"I could forgive much," thought Smith dreamily, "but I cannot forgive this poisoning. Wait a little, M. le Diable!"

HE HAD encountered no one. Nor did he see anyone until noon, when Lebrun in person fetched his tray and regarded him with a thin smile.

"My dear Smith, you have antagonized Félice. This is unfortunate, really!"

"Can't help it," said the American. "Mutual antagonism, I suppose. How's everything?"

The other nodded complacently. "Excellent. Le Morpion procured some brandy, and his wound is inflamed. He'll be around tomorrow, I trust. By the way, you'll join us at dinner tonight? We are a bit short of help, you understand, and since you can walk —"

"By all means," assented Smith. "You are a good surgeon!"

Lebrun bowed, laughed, and departed.

At the dinner table that night, Smith for the first time met Berangère des Gachons. The houeshold arrangements were, in the nature of things, informal. Le Morpion, who possessed some culinary skill, was aiding Félice as cook; Curel buttled, with his tongue in his cheek. At the table in the dining room, which was lighted by two huge candelabra, were only Lebrun, Smith, and the girl.

Berangère appeared clad in black, crowned by her radiant hair; her blue eyes were dimmed by sorrow, her face pale. She was silent and unsmiling, yet by the quiet manner in which she assumed her position of hostess, Smith was entirely convinced that this game was to be played out here on the spot — there was to be no running away!

The introduction had been performed mechanically; the talk was all in French. But, when at the table, Smith made a passing remark to Lebrun in English. Instantly he found the blue eyes of the girl widening upon him, a new light stirring in their depths. She leaned forward.

"Pardon, monsieur — is not your name Smith? You are an American?"

Smith smiled and assented. But the girl said no more; she relapsed into her silence, and betrayed slight interest in the conversation. Perhaps Lebrun, who missed nothing, perceived that from time to time her gaze dwelt upon Smith in frowning curiosity. The meal over, Berangère bade the others make themselves at home, and excused herself.

Lebrun and Smith settled down to cheroots in the library, where Le Morpion and Curel joined them. Here, presently, came Félice with word that Berangère had retired for the night.

"And," she added, lighting a cigarette and settling into a chair, "I have had enough of being a maid, me! How much longer, Paul, before —"

She broke off significantly. Lebrun gave Smith a glance, and his thin smile.

"M. Smith can hardly become a bridegroom as yet," he responded. "Unless, that is, he prefers to arrange matters with the young lady in advance —"

"Don't you worry about me," said Smith. "It's settled that the girl belongs to me?"

He saw Curel wince slightly. Le Morpion grinned. Lebrun nodded assent.

"Then I'll have a talk with her tomorrow," said the American. He rose. "I'm off for bed — can't afford to overdo now. Good night!"

"I'll help you," volunteered Curel.

THEY left the room together and sought Smith's bedroom. Neither man spoke until they had closed the door, and Curel had lighted the lamp. Then, blowing out the match, he looked at the American and smiled in his melancholy way.

"You can't possibly mean," he said questioningly, "that you'll strike tomorrow?"

Smith nodded. "It'll have to be now or never, Curel. Late tomorrow afternoon, perhaps. I'll have a talk with Berangère." He broke into a quick laugh, "What's so terrible about it, after all? The odds are absolutely even. A woman against a woman. A wounded man against a wounded man. You against Lebrun. Bah!"

Curel fingered his beard. His dark eyes were somber.

"You mistake," he answered. "It is not so at all. It

is Berangère against Félice; you against Le Morpion; and I — I! — against M. le Diable. Well, we shall see!"

With this rather cryptic utterance, he departed.

When Smith wakened to the early morning sunlight in his room, he felt himself again — only the twinge of pain as he left the bed, brought him to realization that he was good for little. Still, the weakness had gone. He dressed with cheerful confidence in himself, and went down to breakfast. When Berangère appeared he saw that she, too, seemed more like the girl she must have been. He wished vaguely that he had known her before this blow had stricken her.

He had already decided that Berangère must attend to Félice. Woman against woman.

During breakfast, Smith discovered that there was something amiss with his bandage, which had slipped. After the meal he returned to his room, adjusted the binding firmly, pocketed his automatic, and resolved to have a talk with Berangère at once.

Yet the house seemed oddly deserted. Before speaking with the girl, he must assure himself that the others were out of the way; but he could not find them. He went to the kitchen. Le Morpion had vanished. Curel and Lebrun were nowhere.

In the hall, Smith paused before a rack of sticks. His eye was caught by a fine Malacca, and for this he discarded the heavier stick which he had been using. Then he perceived that the Malacca was a sword-cane — three-edged, elegant, deadly, its triangular blade finely chased. He took this, and then turned at a step behind him.

It was Berangère. She was dressed for the pool, a light wrap about her shoulders, cloaking her gold-clad figure.

She paused at sight of him, and her blue eyes flashed.

"Mademoiselle, I was about to seek you," said Smith, "in order to beg a few moments —"

"Perhaps you will reconsider," said she, coldly, "when I tell you that I know you."

"What?" Smith's brows lifted. "I am afraid —"

"No protestations, if you please," she broke in. "I am aware that there is a reward for you. I am also aware that, a year or so ago, you were the confidential emissary of the governor-general himself; I have remembered your face at last. You are the man who reorganized the police system. You are the man who tracked down the opium traffic from Yunnan and stamped it out. You are the man who broke up the criminal gangs along the western border.

"For all this, monsieur, you have received recognition. I find you here, shipwrecked and hurt; you are welcome to shelter and food. But, I pray you, seek nothing more! I know that the governor-general himself offers a thousand dollars for information as to your whereabouts.

"What crimes you have committed, how you have fallen so low from so high a place, I do not know nor do I desire to know. Kindly remember, monsieur, that I wish no intrusion."

Smith was absolutely taken aback. Before he could find words to respond, Berangère had turned to the doorway and was gone. He stared after her, and swore under his breath.

An evil chuckle startled him.

He turned, to see Le Morpion in the library doorway, standing there and grinning at him.

"So! I begin to comprehend a few things," said Le Morpion ominously.

CHAPTER VIII

Le Morpion Comprehends Everything

"I BEGIN to comprehend why L'Etoile died," said Le Morpion, his baleful grin still fastened upon the American. His head was thrust forward, his small eyes glittering.

The two men stood, thus, at gaze. Le Morpion produced no weapon.

It was clear that he considered Smith unarmed; he himself, doubtless, had appropriated Smith's automatic.

"Don't make a mistake," said Smith calmly.

"Not I. You stated, I believe, that you were some sort of engineer, at work on the new railroad construction? Very good. Yet this girl recognizes you as the man of whom we all heard, yet whom no one knew — the man whom the governor-general trusted."

"You forget," drawled Smith, "the slight matter of my being at present wanted by the authorities."

Le Morpion shook his head.

"I forget nothing, me! I don't forget, for instance, that you are the unknown foreigner who has played the devil with all honest thieves — the mysterious foreigner! Well, there is no more mystery."

"There is no more mystery," murmured Smith, with a slight nod of assent. "That is all very true, Le Morpion. But now I am your comrade."

Le Morpion laughed harshly.

"My comrade? Bah! I don't forget that L'Etoile was

my comrade. As for you, assassin, you are no comrade of mine! I want no policeman at my side."

"But, the reward —"

Le Morpion brushed aside this suggestion with a shake of his bulging jaws.

"No, no! Never mind all that." He leered at Smith, brought up his hands, and began to crack his warped knuckles rapidly. "Hey! Do you know that I am going to kill you?"

Smith gazed at him with imperturbable calm. Only his right thumb moved, very slightly. With this movement, he unfastened the catch which would lay bare the steel of the sword-cane in his hand. "Kill me?" he repeated. "But, in the name of everything, why?"

Le Morpion laughed. From him emanated a faint but distinct reek; obviously, he had been at the brandy bottle again. He was not responsible.

Smith perceived that there could be but one issue from this encounter. He could read this issue in the eyes of the other man. Le Morpion knew him to be wounded, weakened, and unarmed. There was no pity in the eyes of the killer.

ALMOST instantly Smith dismissed the notion of shooting Le Morpion. He could do it with ease; but a shot at this juncture would spoil everything. A shot would bring everyone, and there must be no shooting until the time was ripe. Le Morpion was merely an obstacle; the true focus of danger was Monsieur the Devil. And for all Smith knew, Lebrun might be in the adjoining room.

"Kill me?" he said again. "Why?"

"In the first place, because you killed poor L'Etoile," grated Le Morpion, coming a step or two closer. A new gleam lightened his evil eyes. "And, in the second place, because I have decided that this girl shall be mine instead of yours. In the third place, because you are the mysterious foreigner. I don't like foreigners, me, nor mystery either!"

"But," argued Smith pleasantly, "all this is no basis for killing, my friend! Besides, M. le Diable wishes to make use of me."

Le Morpion leered. "Yes, but when he learns who you are, he may change his mind!"

"At least, you will allow me to die quickly?"

"As quickly as my hands will do it." Le Morpion bared his teeth. "Ah! You damned gentlemen — I want to feel your throats under my thumbs! Curel is another, with his accursed lazy elegance. Well, his turn will come! Now I shall kill you."

"In effect, you understand everything?" said Smith.

"Everything!" repeated the other, drawing closer, his hands outstretched and tense. In his eyes was the blood-lust.

"But there is one mystery which you do not yet comprehend," said Smith very calmly.

The other paused, blinking at him.

"Eh? And what is that, you white-throat?"

"The mystery of life and death. I shall endeavor to elucidate it."

As he spoke, Smith moved.

His foot struck the thigh of Le Morpion — struck that wounded thigh which had been sewed by Lebrun. It was a shrewd kick, carrying very little force, but with enough to serve its purpose quite well.

From Le Morpion was wrenched a cry of agony. He doubled up, catching with both hands at his wounded thigh. Before he could move again, Smith had whipped the thin triangular blade from its malacca sheath and lunged forward with it. The thrust went home just as Le Morpion was straightening up.

The blade entered at the collar-bone, and Le Morpion, rising as though to meet that deadly thrust, impaled himself. The blade protruded a foot behind his shoulder. He caught at the hilt with both hands, and his mouth opened. Like an orang-outang shot through the chest, who claws at the wound and foams great screams of fury, Le Morpion tore at the thin blade and tried to vent his rage — but no sound came from him. His mouth gasped frightfully. He tried to rush forward upon Smith, but death was loosening his knees.

"I believe," said Smith coolly, "that at last you comprehend everything, my friend?"

The eyes of Le Morpion widened. He clutched at the air, and rocked upon his feet for an instant; then his knees doubled, and he fell backward through the doorway of the library, whence he had emerged. Smith stepped forward and closed the door, and turned back to the rack of sticks.

"Thank you for the sword-cane, M. des Gachons!" he said. "Your gardener is avenged."

Selecting another stick, this one of green ebony, he left the house.

His first intent was to follow Berangère, who had evidently gone to the swimming pool. Then he paused, and turned.

Whither had Lebrun gone? Where else than to the little harbor in which lay the boats?

Smith decided quickly, and started for the cove. Before he had taken two steps, he put a hand to his side and sank down. That quick, swift lunge had hurt his wound.

He sat on a step of the portico, there in the sunlight, and cursed softly. Admission was forced upon him that the odds were heavy — heavier than he had reckoned. After all, there was something in the sardonic suggestion of Curel that by the time he came to deal with Lebrun he would be very nearly dead!

This thought drew a twisted smile to his lips.

After a moment he writhed out of his jacket, and opened his shirt. It was not so bad as he had feared; the wound had not been reopened after all. Still, the skin had received a shrewd pull.

"Another such jolt will finish me," he reflected.

He got into his jacket again and leaned back, feeling a bit sick. Presently he took out his pipe and tobacco, and smoked. At a sudden thought, he produced the automatic which Curel had brought him, and examined it.

To his utter dismay, he found that it contained but a single cartridge, that in the firing chamber. There was no clip underneath. He put it back into his pocket and stared at the green trees, his eyes hard and cold.

"The cards, it seems, run worse every minute," he said to himself. "Lebrun, you are well called! You have the luck of the very devil himself!"

He might find a weapon on the body of Le Morpion, but he dared not risk the effort of going to get it. Every ounce of strength left to him, must be stored and saved. Every iota of energy was precious in the extreme.

Two courses were open to him. In one direction, at the end of that avenue of palms, was Berangère; he might go to her. In the other direction was the harbor, where he might join Curel and Lebrun. Why not go thither, and attend to M. le Diable at once? He would have Curel to help.

This was the better course, decidedly.

He knocked out his pipe and rose. After a moment he stood leaning on the stick, and turned toward the cove. It occurred to him with passing curiosity that he had seen nothing of Félice Bonnard, but he dismissed the thought as inconsequential. She was probably about the house somewhere.

HOLDING himself stiffly, Smith slowly proceeded toward the harbor. He could walk well enough, although his strength was slender. What worried him most was the single cartridge in his automatic. It gave him a terribly slim margin.

Pausing occasionally to rest, he followed the winding path and came, at last, to the little house perched at the verge of the cliff overlooking the cove. He had already heard from the others of the counter-balanced weights and the moving escalier, and knew how it was worked. There was only a lever to pull.

He sank down upon the seat overlooking the cove. For a moment he felt dizzy and weak; everything was a blur. Then a voice and a step, and the creak of the escalier; he looked up to see Lebrun standing before him.

"Smith! What's the matter, man?" exclaimed the other quickly. "You're livid —"

Smith's fingers trembled. One cartridge! He dared not do it now. He could not trust himself to shoot.

"Overdone," he said, faintly. "Hurt my side."

"Rest," said Lebrun with decision. "Take it easy, man! I've been working here this morning. Make yourself at home — the place is yours."

With a chuckle, he passed on.

Smith looked after him, and even reached for his pocket. Then he paused. He dared not risk that one cartridge — he could not put faith in his hand at this moment. Then the moment was passed; Lebrun had disappeared.

With a long breath, Smith regained control of himself. The weakness passed. It was very good to sit here and rest. His eyes wandered to the cove beneath — ah! What was wrong down there?

He leaned forward, alert once more. He saw now what it was that Lebrun had been working over, doubtless aided by Curel. All those boats down there had vanished. Only one remained: the large motor cruiser, which had been drawn in to the boathouse, where the water was deep close to the float.

"He took them out and sank them — beyond the reef!" murmured Smith. "But where is Curel?"

A vague but terrible uneasiness laid hold upon him. He rose, peering downward. A moving shape caught his eye; he saw Félice Bonnard appear for an instant at the after hatchway of the motor cruiser. Her head came into sight, then vanished again.

But what of Curel? He was not in sight.

The lips of Smith drew into a thin line. He rose, leaned for a moment on his stick, then stepped to the escalier. A touch of the lever, and he was being taken swiftly downward.

CHAPTER IX

One Cannot Escape the Devil

STANDING on the shore, Smith looked about. Curel was not in sight anywhere, but the door of the boat-house stood wide open; one passed through this to the float beyond, where was moored the motor cruiser. After a minute Smith approached the boathouse. Félice Bonnard appeared to be very busy aboard the cruiser. Upon the float Smith saw a pile of cases and miscellaneous stuff, doubtless the cargo removed from the smaller cruiser before she had been sunk.

Lebrun's object in sinking the other craft was clear enough. There would be the big cruiser remaining, in which everything could be carried away that was worth while. In the meantime, neither Berangère nor anyone else would be able to leave. Doubtless Lebrun meant to guard that big cruiser night and day.

"And when I had served his purpose, had accomplished his final revenge for him upon the Des Gachons family," thought Smith, "he would calmly depart, leave me here, and send the authorities after me! And I would be taken as the criminal responsible for the whole business. Not a bad scheme, except that —"

He broke off, smiling thinly.

Now the motor cruiser and float were out of his sight, as he came near the boat-house. It did not occur to him that anything might have happened, down here. His uneasiness was purely subconscious. Yet he remembered the terrible sang-froid of Lebrun, which was most apparent at times of stress, and he hastened his lagging steps.

Félice, he reflected, was no doubt at work on something in the hold of the cruiser, and Curel was with her. Monsieur the Devil had probably gone in search of Le Morpion, for at this juncture all hands counted. Well, let him search! The one cartridge still remained.

So thinking, Smith entered the open doorway of the boathouse. Opposite him, the door giving on the float was also open. The interior of the building was well lighted. Smith came to a sudden halt and stared at Curel, who sat on a pile of rope just inside the door. Curel was wiping his lips with the back of his hand, as though he had just been drinking; but the back of his hand came away red.

"So, you have come!" said Curel in a faint voice.

"Obviously," returned Smith. "See here! What's the matter with you —"

Curel looked up, with a shadow of his melancholy smile.

"Nothing," he said quietly, "except that I am dying. I had a chance to get Lebrun — but before I could do it, that she-devil had stabbed me through the back. I'm done, Smith. There's one thing you can do — quickly! Go out and clap on the hatch — prison her in the hold — do it quickly! I'll be dead in half an hour — let me still do what I can —"

SMITH stood motionless for an instant, shocked into immobility. It came to him in a flash that Curel still had some scheme, some plan — the man was dying, yet his brain was at work! Without response, the American stepped forward and came out on the float, to which the big cruiser was moored.

He paused. A step or two on the deck, and Félice would have warning. Quietly as possible, he followed the rail of the cruiser aft, then gathered himself and gained the deck. Two swift steps took him to the after hatchway, which was open. The hatch lay beside the opening.

Stooping, Smith seized the cover and dragged it into place. As it fell, a muffled exclamation came from below. A coil of rope lay neatly flaked to one side. Smith caught hold of this, drew it to the hatch, and dumped it on top. The hatch lifted a little to pressure from below; Smith stepped on it and waited, resting, panting a little as he leaned on his cane. He smiled, and listened to a storm of furious imprecations from the imprisoned woman.

After a moment, satisfied that the coil of rope would be more than Félice could move, the American turned and retraced his steps. Entering the boathouse, he found Curel up on his feet, wavering and clinging to the wall for support. He caught the man's arm. Curel shook off his hand with petulant impatience.

"Be quiet!" Curel's eyes were feverish and terrible. "Do what I tell you —"

"Have you a weapon?" demanded Smith. "There was only one cartridge in the pistol you brought me."

Curel gazed at him and uttered a hollow laugh.

"None. Lebrun took mine. They — they brushed me aside as one brushes a maimed insect! But that was a mistake. I can still — here! Help me outside —"

Smith aided him to walk. Slowly and painfully, Curel gained the rail of the boat, and with a terrible effort came to the deck. He stumbled and fell, gasping blood. Smith helped him up again.

"I attended to Le Morpion," he said quietly.

"Good! There will remain — only M. le Diable. He will kill you, but what matter? It is for the girl, the sweet girl!" Curel caught his breath. "Well, at least I shall die like a poet! Into the pilot house —"

Smith guided his feeble steps. Presently the two men came into the wheel-house, and at a gasped order, Smith drew a wicker chair before the helm. Curel sank into this.

"We were running the boat — towing the others out — sinking them. Go and start the engine. The switches are set. The — the white button will start —"

THE American went aft to the engine-room. From below was coming a frantic pounding; he could hear Félice crying out, her voice muffled and desperate. Some inkling of Curel's scheme came to him as he touched the buttons and heard the engines throb into sudden life. He came back to Curel, who was testing the controls, and who greeted him with another smile.

"Now, my friend," gasped Curel, who was white as death, "cast off the lines! We shall go out to sea, this Félice and I; and perhaps a week hence, they will find Des Gachons' boat with a dead man still guiding it westward — after all, it is the best way! One cannot shoot a woman. And it is for the sake of the sweet girl — Holy Virgin, will you hurry? I am dying fast!"

Smith stumbled away, unable to speak. Once on the float, he made shift to cast off the lines. He caught the voice of Curel lifting to him, so faintly that the words were lost; then the engines hummed, and the motor cruiser darted from the float.

The American stood gazing after it. He was still numbed by that final outburst of authority from Curel — the frenzied pleading of the dying man! Now, as he watched the boat draw out, he marveled at it all. There was no craft left here in which he might escape with Berangère; yet what need? Curel was gone, dying, and with him he was taking Félice. The boat would be surely picked up sooner or later, and recognized.

As for Félice, Smith gave her not a thought. She was gone, that was all.

His eyes following the lessening boat, Smith wondered how long Curel would live to hold her. Straight as an arrow, she was leaping out from the island toward the horizon. Suddenly he saw her veer, waver drunkenly, then pick up a new course. He turned away, his lips set hard. He knew what had happened then.

His lips curved in a grim smile as he walked along. What a desperate game in which destiny seemed to deal the cards!

He had one cartridge, and very little strength.

Even had it been otherwise — even had he been well armed, in possession of all his old strength and skill and cool confidence, he would have found Monsieur the Devil a terrible antagonist. But now —

Smith lifted his head and smiled to himself. Well, with all the cards stacked, the game remained to be played! Win or lose, the game remained! Could he gain the help of Berangère, there might be a chance. And, instead of depending upon cartridges which were not, there were other things just as dependable — inward things, things of the soul and brain and cool eyes! After all, he was in this affair for the thrill of the game itself!

So he came to the house, and, because he doubted his ability to waste much strength, he lifted his voice and called Lebrun.

There was no response. Twice more Smith called the man's name, but received no answer. The house remained silent. Smith hesitated, then turned to the avenue of palms. Just as well, perhaps! He must find Berangère — and tell her the truth.

Slowly, drawing carefully upon his low vitality, Smith made his way along that shady avenue, and came upon the sky-blue pool at the end, with its circle of white sand and its wall. He paused, for Berangère was not here. The canvas awning shaded only white sand. What? Surely she could not have returned to the house?

Then he perceived the gate in the wall, and that this gate stood open. Coming to it he rested a moment. Before him was outspread the little orchard. Twenty feet away, stretched out beneath a flame-tree, was Berangère. She lay motionless, with her face in her arms.

Smith closed the gate and came forward. The girl stirred, glanced up, then rose lithely. Her eyes were angry as she spoke.

"Monsieur! How dare you —"

"Be quiet, please," said Smith calmly. "You must listen to me; I have information for you which is vital and terrible. I regret that I must cause you great grief, mademoiselle; but your father did not die of ptomaine or other causes. He was murdered."

As she regarded him, the girl went white as death.

"I know that," she said in a low voice. Smith started.

"What? You say —"

"I guessed as much, since the letter he supposedly left for me was palpably forged." Her voice was icy. "Also, you, a criminal, were here. And —"

Smith checked her with upraised hand.

"I am not a criminal," he said quietly. "Let me speak, please — minutes may be valuable! Do you remember a man whom your father sent to Noumea for life — a rather notorious person who was called M. le Diable?"

"I have heard something of him, yes," she answered.

"That man is Lebrun, with whom you breakfasted this morning. Your maid Félice is one of his accomplices. So is — or was — Le Morpion. So, presumably, were Curel and I. But Curel was a gentleman. We were not aware of what Lebrun intended here; I shot one of the gang en route, and was wounded, prostrated. You understand all this?"

She was staring from wide, stricken eyes.

"I was unable to prevent what happened," went on Smith. "In order to save you, Curel and I decided to strike without delay. I killed Le Morpion this morning; but your maid, Félice, murdered Curel. Still, Félice has been attended to. There now remains Lebrun, M. le Diable himself. Against him I can do little. I am feeble, and I must depend on you to get me a weapon — a pistol, you understand? If we work together —"

"Wait!" Berangère brushed one hand across her eyes, then looked at Smith as though she had expected to see him vanish, dream-like. "You say — you are no criminal —"

"I am not," said Smith. "Some time ago I learned that a number of M. le Diable's gang were at large, and got a clue to them. I followed that clue, and was about to have them arrested when M. le Diable himself turned up, having escaped from Noumea. After that I was given no opportunity to bring about an arrest until we had left Saigon and it was too late —"

"But — the — reward —"

"Was offered," and Smith smiled, "in the hope that it would remove suspicion from me, in case I were recognized —"

"Oh!" A cry broke from the girl. "You — how do I know this is not some frightful lie —"

A third voice interrupted, broke in upon them with suave insistence.

"I assure you that it is the truth, mademoiselle," said Monsieur the Devil, as he rose from the pomegranate hedge and approached them, smiling his thin smile.

CHAPTER X

The One Shot

"IT IS the absolute truth, mademoiselle," repeated Lebrun, advancing. "I shall presently offer proof, by killing this excellent policeman and attempting to console you in person. Please sit down and do not interrupt us, mademoiselle. Now, M. Smith, will you throw away that stick, and seat yourself? Thus I shall be able to dispense with this heavy weapon, for a time." He indicated the automatic in his hand.

Smith, whose face had reddened with chagrin and the astounded sense that all was lost, threw away his cane and sank down upon the grass. Evidently Lebrun considered him unarmed, especially from his recent words to Berangère.

There was a moment of silence. Lebrun came forward, put his weapon into his pocket, and drew out a cheroot, which he lighted. Berangère drew the silk wrap closer about her, staring from wide eyes, filled with fright and terror and comprehension of her own situation. Smith, thinking of that single cartridge in his pocket, looked at the cliff-edge and the sea; and in this moment there came to him the idea of poetic retribution. When he looked back at Lebrun, he was smiling.

"I may smoke?" he asked calmly. Lebrun nodded.

"Certainly — your last smoke, M. Smith. I know, of course, that you will die well." Smith put his hand into his pocket, and pulled out pipe and tobacco. He filled and lighted the pipe, bringing matches from his pocket.

"If you had not taken the pistol from my clothes —" he said significantly.

"Le Morpion did that. You killed Le Morpion this morning, I believe you said?"

"Yes. And Félice has gone to sea with Curel at the helm of the ship."

At this, Lebrun showed a trifle of astonishment. Then he slowly smiled.

"Well, that is not so bad!" he declared cheerfully. "So Félice is gone? Then she will not be here to interfere, if I attempt to console Mlle. des Gachons! That is excellent! And I must congratulate you, M. Smith, upon the way you fooled me in Saigon. And if L'Etoile had not stabbed you, I almost believe that you would have prevented the demise of M. des Gachons!"

"Certainly," responded Smith. "You will remember that, after the moment we arrived, I never saw him again. Otherwise, I should certainly have warned him —"

A low moan broke from Berangère. Horror sat in her eyes, which were fastened on Lebrun.

"You — then are you the man —"

Lebrun bowed slightly. "I am the man, my dear. M. le Diable, at your service presently! First I must take care of this impertinent policeman. We three, I gather, are alone on the island. Now history repeats itself, M. Smith! So you are what is called a detective?"

"I am many things," said Smith calmly.

Berangère moved. The silk wrap fell from about her shoulders, and she lay quiet. She had finally realized that she was talking with the man who had murdered her father — and she had fainted.

"That is excellent," said Lebrun, taking the pistol from his pocket. "Suppose, my dear Smith, that you rise and take a little walk! Let us approach the edge of the cliff."

With a gesture of resignation, Smith managed to rise. For an instant he stood, one hand pressed against his wound. Then he drew a deep breath, took the pipe from his mouth, and knocked it out against the palm of his hand.

"I suppose," he asked, casually, "there is no chance of buying my life?"

"My dear fellow, don't be silly!" Lebrun's eyes glittered venomously. "I have always intended to shape events so that, in the end, this charming bit of girlhood would be mine," and he gestured toward the inert figure of Berangère, lying like a wilted golden flower. "You see, it was at this very spot I first came out of the sea, and —"

"Then," said Smith, putting his pipe into his pocket, "it is obviously only proper that at this point you should go back into the sea —"

And, as he spoke, he fired the one cartridge.

Lebrun whirled about. The pistol flew from his hand. The hand itself dropped to his side, broken and mangled in red confusion. Smith covered the man with his empty weapon and spoke:

"Come here!"

Writhing under the agony of that mangled hand, Lebrun obeyed. His face was frightful to look upon. He spat at Smith a low vitriolic stream of curses.

"That's enough!" commanded Smith sharply. "Turn your back."

Lebrun hesitated, then obeyed, so that he was facing the cliff.

"Now mind your step, my man," said Smith quietly, his voice like steel. "I don't intend to guard you, I don't intend to take you back to Saigon, and I don't intend to kill you. If you force a bullet, I shall shoot you in the abdomen — you comprehend? That is all."

Stooping, Smith picked up the silk wrap of the girl and threw it over the shoulder of Lebrun.

"Put that over your head and walk forward," he commanded. "You shall return to the sea whence you came. If you do not relish that program, then you may force a bullet — but in such an event, I warn you, the result will be most unpleasant and lingering. Choose!"

In THE gray eyes of Smith, M. le Diable read absolutely no mercy. Probably he expected none. His fate lay clear before him. At his side, his right hand dripped blood. None the less, despite this mangled hand, despite the unexpected turn which had so swiftly overwhelmed him, Lebrun smiled. In his manner was a power, a singular indomitable majesty.

"You will never be a great man, Smith," he observed, "because you have a sense of humor. I have none; that is why I am what I am. And do you think that you can end the life of Monsieur the Devil? Des Gachons thought so, when he sent me to Noumea; but I came back from the dead."

"Go at once," said Smith coldly.

"Very well, monsieur. But may I be permitted to say *au revoir?*"

With this, Lebrun walked deliberately toward the cliff. He did not glance backward. He came to the verge, and for one instant stood there, outlined against the sky and sea. The next instant — he was gone.

Like an echo from hell, his thin laugh floated upward.

Smith, trembling, picked up his cane and made his way to the cliff edge. He gazed downward. There was nothing in sight. The green water swirled below in faint whiteness against the rocks.

Smith tossed his empty pistol into the sea, and turned. "A good game, well played!" he said, and sighed. "Yet, perhaps I should have shot him and made certain! But we'll find his body washing on the rocks tomorrow."

His eyes fell on the figure of Berangère, and they softened.

"Well, it's finished!" His voice sounded very faint and distant in his ears. "And now — and now — the rest is up to you, mademoiselle — up to you — and Curel!"

He lay quietly upon the grass, and his eyes closed.

The End

www.ingramcontent.com/pod-product-compliance
Lightning Source LLC
Chambersburg PA
CBHW032206190626
46810CB00018B/1889